Flawed

Damaged Hearts book 2

Margaux Paris

Flawed

Flawed

Paperback ISBN: 978-1-7643194-5-4

Please note: British English spelling has been used throughout this book.

Book design by Margaux Paris
Cover design by Margaux Paris
Edited by CJ Editing

First Edition: March 2025

Flawed

DEDICATION

This story isn't for the faint of hearts- or the firmly law- abiding. It's for the readers who see the warning signs and whisper,
"I can fix him."

Who knows that healing isn't always clean, love isn't always kind, and sometimes, the villain just needs the right girl to hand him the match.

Flawed

Trigger Warning

Flawed contains mature themes and content that may be distressing to some readers. This includes references to sexual assault, emotional manipulation, psychological trauma, toxic relationships, obsessive behaviour, and mental health struggles.
The story is intended for adult readers and explores complex, often confronting emotional dynamics.
Please read with care.

Flawed

Authors Note

Flawed is the direct continuation of *Broken*, the first book in the *Damaged Hearts Duet*. This story is not intended to be read as a standalone. To fully understand the characters, their history, and the emotional depth of their journey, please read *Broken* first.

This is a duet about love, obsession, trauma, and the mess we make in trying to survive them.

This is where it ends—raw, ruined, and real.

Flawed

Flawed

Playlist

Popular Monster- **Falling in Reverse**

Voices in My Head - **Falling in Reverse**

Zombified - **Falling in Reverse**

The Drug In Me Is You - **Falling in Reverse**

Wicked Game – **Ursine Vulpine ft. Annaca**

Love the Way You Lie (Part II) – **Rihanna**

I Wanna Be Your Slave – **Måneskin**

Beggin' – **Måneskin**

Freak Like Me – **Halestorm**

Take Me to Church – **Hozier**

Play with Fire – **Sam Tinnesz**

Scream my name – **Thomas LaRosa**

Flawed

CHAPTER 1

JAX

Get your fucking shit together.

My brain is screaming at my body, but it's not getting the message. My stomach keeps heaving into my throat.

I've spent the last fifteen minutes hunched over the toilet, dry-retching bile thanks to a week of barely eating. My body is finally cracking, trying to purge whatever poison's been festering inside. Slumped against the tiles opposite the toilet, I struggle to make sense of what the fuck is happening to me.

People like me don't feel guilt. They don't feel remorse. And they sure as hell don't feel empathy. We lie, manipulate, and set fire to the social rulebook to get what we want. So why the fuck does it feel like regret is clawing its way through my chest? This feeling is going to swallow me whole, stew me in its acid, then spit me out and take a piss on the remains.

I've never felt anything like this. But I guess anyone's first run-in with actual emotion would knock them sideways.

Twenty-four years of ice-cold detachment, and now I'm sucker-punched by what, an emotionally unstable woman with trauma issues? It's fucking ridiculous.

The whole thing's laughable. Yet here I am, leaning on the fucking bathroom wall, struggling to breathe under the weight of something I don't even understand. Maybe guilt? Is that what this is? Fucking hell.

My name's Jax Beckett, and I'm no longer a psychopath.

Fuck. I can almost hear the imaginary support group

in my head echoing, *Hi, Jax.*

I drag myself off the wall, grip the sink, and stare into the mirror. The bastard looking back is a wreck—hollow eyes, shadowed from a week of no sleep, beard overgrown, skin a sickly shade of grey-green. Lucky I can work from home this week—there's no energy left to fake giving a fuck.

Took years to perfect my craft. Out there, I'm perfect—funny, considerate, charming, an all around nice guy. I can't help but snort at the irony of it. Behind the curtain? I'm a deceitful, manipulative cunt with anger issues and zero empathy for others. I'm a damn good actor, having learned early on that playing a role gives me the upper hand. People are easier to manipulate when they don't see the real me coming. Life was smooth sailing until this train wreck of a woman barged in, and now I've caught feelings like they're some kind of contagious disease.

I've been parking outside her apartment every night like a deranged creep, engine off, lights out, just sitting there. Watching. Waiting. Making sure she's safe—or at least that's the lie I tell myself.

I don't knock. Don't call. Just sit in my car like some obsessed freak, convincing myself that distance makes it okay. It doesn't. I'm no better than the monster she's running from. I might even be worse. At least *he* didn't pretend to care.

The doorbell rings, but I keep berating the stranger in the mirror until it rings again. Only one person would be that fucking persistent and I don't want him seeing me like this.

Then the bell goes berserk—he's holding it down like the annoying prick he is.

I splash water on my face and head downstairs. That's when I hear the sharp crack of glass.

Brilliant.

"You broke my fucking window."

"Jesus, you look like you're dying."

"Thanks, dickhead. I've got the flu. You better piss off before you catch it."

"Not a chance. You haven't answered your phone in a week. I thought you were dead. You still might be, by the looks of you."

I flip him the bird and head to the kitchen, grabbing

the bourbon I couldn't stomach last night. One gulp down—I'm gonna need it.

I turn, offer him the bottle. He eyes it like it's radioactive.

"It's 9:30 in the morning."

"And?"

"And people with the flu don't drink bourbon like it's Hydralyte. What's really going on?"

Ollie's biggest flaw is that he gives a shit. Poor bastard cares too much. He insists that it's normal, but I have my doubts. He sees me as both a brother and a friend, which is fine; it's nice to know someone's got your back, even if you don't reciprocate. He's been a constant in my life, always forgiving me for the torture I put him through as a kid. He'll tell you the worst thing I ever did to him was open the backyard gate and watch the family dog run away, or when I fucked his girlfriend in the arse on his bed. But that's only because he doesn't know they were some of the nicer things I put him through. Needless to say, that ended pets and girlfriends under Mum and Dad's roof. But he got over it.

If I could care about anyone, it'd be him. But, truth

is, if he caught flesh-eating bacteria tomorrow, I wouldn't blink.

So what hope does *she* have?

Is that why you're still thinking about her?

Fuck you, subconscious. Eat shit and die!

His gaze burns a hole through me as I swig again. The bourbon's warmth crawls down my throat like comfort.

"Jax, how're you meant to work today?"

"Hopefully, drunk off my arse."

He rolls his eyes, then lunges forward, catching me off guard and snatches the bottle.

"Oi! That's mine!"

"Finders keepers." He smirks.

"What are you, six?"

"This got anything to do with that project I met a few weeks ago?"

I snort.

"She still not giving it up? Finally found a woman you can't manipulate?" He teases.

"Fuck you very much. I was balls-deep in her traumatised cunt just last week."

He freezes.

"What do you mean traumatised?"

"She's a 'survivor,'" I say, watching his face turn white.

Bingo! That'll teach him to steal my bourbon.

"Please tell me that's a sick joke only you think is funny."

"What do you mean?" I'm not joking, but if he thinks I am, I want to know why. Humour has always been tricky—I understand the concept, but it was the most challenging thing for me to master.

"I think I'm going to be sick."

"Well, you should've left when you had the chance. Welcome to the flu."

Glass shatters against the floor. The last bottle. Cheers, cunt.

"Please tell me you didn't target a fucking assault survivor for one of your twisted games!"

I shrug.

"WHAT THE ACTUAL FUCK IS WRONG WITH YOU?"

And now we're shouting.

"THIS IS THE MOST FUCKED UP THING YOU'VE

EVER DONE!"

"Oh, come on. Don't be dramatic. Remember when I shoved that girl down the stairs in high school 'cause she said she was pregnant?"

He opens his mouth. Shuts it.

"You're right. That was worse. But this is a close second!"

He's red in the face now, fists clenched.

"Why, Jax? Why'd you do it?"

"Didn't want the baby. And she was lying, anyway."

"No, you fucking arsehole—I meant the other thing."

"I dunno. To prove I could? And stop looking at me like that. I feel bad enough already."

That makes him pause. His posture eases, and it dawns on me just how badly I've fucked up.

"You do?" his voice softens. I stare at the floor, shoulders tense. Another shrug.

"Oh, how the mighty have fallen. That's it, isn't it? You feel guilty."

Another shrug.

"Use your words, Jackson and I'll buy you a new bottle."

"Fine! Yes, I feel guilty. Happy now? What's next—want me to say I miss her?"

What the fuck did I just say? My impulses are out of control from sleep deprivation and these *emotions* running through my body like fucking cancer.

"Do you?"

Shrug.

"Well, I'll be damned. You're human after all."

"Go fuck yourself."

I push past him then add, "And go get my bourbon!" As I storm up the stairs two at a time and slam the door behind me like a sulky teenager.

CHAPTER 2

ALLY

Day 9 After Jax.

That's how I've been marking time lately. Not with dates or projects—but by the number of days since he left. It's pathetic, I know. But it's how I'm surviving. There's a before him version of me, a with him version, and now this one—after. The aftermath. The wreckage.

Flawed

Before I met Jax, I was… functional, barely. Anxious. Suspicious of everyone. Always waiting for the rug to be pulled out from under me. I existed, sure, but I wasn't really living. Then he came along, and something in me cracked open. For the first time in years, I felt warm inside. Light. Like I could maybe be someone again. Someone who trusted. Someone who loved.

He saw me. Really saw me. And that was terrifying and exhilarating.

But now? Now I feel like a cautionary tale. Some tragic girl in a book you scream at because she should've seen it coming. I'm confused, gutted, humiliated, and too damn proud to admit how deeply this has broken me.

It took me two days just to peel myself off the floor of my bedroom. Not even metaphorically, I mean, literally. I laid there on the carpet, tangled in a t-shirt that smelled like him, with swollen eyes and zero dignity, trying to figure out what the hell happened. By day four, I finally managed to shuffle down the hallway to get the mail like some ghost haunting her own apartment. By day six, I felt anger flicker. It didn't last, but it was there, a tiny, sharp thing, poking at my insides. And by day eight, I decided feeling nothing was better than feeling everything.

So here I am, day nine. Somewhere between denial and depression, drinking instant coffee that tastes like punishment and staring blankly at the edits I'm supposed to be making. The manuscript is revolting—involving multiple disembowelments that the main character shoves into a piñata in preparation for his best friend's birthday party. I officially need a break and to wash my brain out with bleach but its a reprieve to bury myself in someone else's nightmare instead of facing my own.

At least the piñata has closure.

The nights are the worst. Every time I close my eyes, he's there. Except not him, not anymore. The dreams have changed. It used to be Jax—his face, his voice, the warmth of his touch—but now it's just a faceless figure. Same scenes, same feelings, but his face is blurred out like my subconscious is trying to erase him to protect me. Or maybe it's punishing me. I haven't figured out which yet.

Tyler's been calling every day. I told him on day four that things with Jax were over—used the classic 'irreconcilable differences' line. He was stunned. Confused. Sounded almost hurt, like he'd been rooting for us more than I had. He asked what happened, and I couldn't give him a straight answer because I don't have one. What do you say when the man who made you feel alive just vanishes without warning?

I'm convinced it's about the sex. It has to be. But no matter how much I've scoured the internet, I can't figure out why. I didn't think it would be amazing for him, considering my lack of experience, yet all the online advice confirms we had the logistics right. I thought it was something special, but it seems he had a completely different take on it.

Stupid, isn't it? Believing that something that intimate had to mean more than lust. That maybe it was the beginning of something instead of the end.

I know a more self-assured woman would just march over to his place, knock, and demand answers. I wish I could. I wish I was *that* girl. Confident. Brazen.

Someone who walks into the fire just to feel the heat. But I'm not. I'm terrified. What if I see something I can't unsee? Another woman? Another version of him? The real one?

And truthfully, I don't think I can survive a second rejection. The first one already broke me. A second one might kill whatever parts of me are still left.

So I've made a decision—I'm done with sex. Two experiences. One, traumatic. One, soul crushing. I'm 0 for 2, and frankly, I'm tired of betting on something that only ever bankrupts me.

Around 3pm, I finally give up on work. My brain is fried, my emotions are frayed, and my tolerance for fictional murder is at an all-time low. I email Jeanie— not expecting an immediate reply, just needing to send the words. She's the only one who knows the whole story. The before. The after. The in-between. She's been my anchor through the darkest parts of my life, and even though I'm embarrassed to still be this broken, I know she won't judge me.

She's the one who brought to my attention—"You've been lonely a long time, Ally." I didn't want to believe it. But she was right. I just didn't realise how lonely I was until someone finally looked at me like I wasn't invisible. Like I mattered.

And then he vanished.

I shuffle into the kitchen, still in my sparkly pink sneakers, glitter covered headband and the t-shirt he last held me in. I grab a half-melted chocolate bar from the pantry and start eating it like a lifeline. The sugar barely registers.

My phone buzzes.

A number I don't recognise lights up the screen, and as I tap it open, my breath catches in my throat.

Unknown: What do you consider your most

positive qualities or strengths?

I freeze. Stare. My chest tightens painfully. I should ignore it. I should delete it. But I can't. It might be him. And if it is… why this? Why now?

The question sends a jolt of hope through me, but I quickly dismiss it as a mistake. It could be Jax, or maybe he's passed this game on to someone else just to mess with me. Would he really do that? I mean, anything seems possible now; I never thought he would just disappear without a word.

I've concocted a million excuses for his absence, each one more absurd than the last. Maybe he got an emergency call about his brother getting bitten by a shark on some remote island with no cell service and he had to rush out to donate blood because of their rare blood type. That's a thing, right?

I can picture it—him running off into the wild unknown, saving the day, and leaving me none the wiser. Each excuse is a little more ridiculous than the one before, but they all have one thing in common: they're easier to believe than the truth.

The truth that I don't want to face. The truth that maybe, just maybe, he's gone because he wants to be. Or worse, because I wasn't enough to keep him here.

I hate that my fingers move before my brain catches up.

Ally: Compassion.

It's safe. Distant. No questions. No desperation. I won't beg.

Unknown: What a coincidence, that's mine too 

He has the audacity to flirt? After all this time. After disappearing like I didn't mean a thing. No apology. No explanation. Just… this.

Unknown: No sense of humour today? That's cool, we all have off days. Mine's actually restitution.

What the fuck does that even mean? Is he high? I feel like I'm talking to a different person. Has someone stolen his game and is pretending to be him. That's the only way this makes sense.

Ally: Are you on drugs?

Unknown: No. Never been my thing.

Ally: Should you be?

Unknown: Not to the best of my knowledge.

Ally: FUCK YOU!

Unknown: Well *that* was aggressive.

I hurl my phone across the room and scream. A full-body, primal, aching sound that shreds my throat on the way out. Then I collapse onto my bed, bury my face in a pillow, and sob.

He did this.

He broke me.

Flawed

And now, he's acting like none of it ever mattered

CHAPTER 3

JAX

I convinced myself I wouldn't reach out—that I was indifferent to her situation. But when I saw she was feeling lonely again, my hand went for my phone before I even had a chance to think. A rush of unfamiliar feelings came with it, uninvited and impossible to ignore.

A few weeks back, when I hacked into her email, it

was all about gaining insight into what makes her tick; I wanted to have the upper hand in this twisted game I was playing.

Was it a violation of her privacy? Absolutely.

Did I lose any sleep over it? Not for a second.

I've always thrived in that morally grey space without a hint of guilt, and it's worked out just fine for me. However, things took a turn when I couldn't stop checking her emails after I left her place. Her daily exchanges with her therapist revealed her struggle to figure out what went wrong, and she seemed to think it was about the sex—what a fucking joke!

I almost stormed over to her place to set her straight on that misguided thought, but somehow, I managed to hold myself back.

Truth is, the sex is what has kept me fixated on her even a week and a half later, not the fact that I slipped away while she was asleep. People say emotional connection makes sex better. I used to call bullshit on that. But FUCK, I've never felt anything like her before.

Usually I'm a one-and-done. Box ticked, ego stroked, next. But with Ally I craved a second round. I tried to convince myself that the first time was just a fluke. The incredible feeling of her wrapped around my cock was merely a sense of accomplishment from finally getting inside her. But the second time? It was *better*. That warm, fuzzy feeling in my gut only got stronger the deeper I sank into her.

That night we met, it had nothing to do with her. I just jumped into the conversation to take the piss out of some guy making a fool of himself. But when she zoned out and flinched at my touch, I felt a spark of curiosity. It had been a while since I got to flex my acting muscles, and I wanted to see if I still had it in me.

Sure, I perform daily for colleagues and strangers. But she was different. She gave me a new challenge. It wasn't her I targeted—it was the opportunity to test myself. I didn't need to care about her to be interested. I never do. But when she flinched, I knew something had marked her. I wanted to know what. And yeah, I wanted to fuck her.

The original plan was to vanish after I got inside her, but this strange feeling—I now recognise as guilt— made me grab a pen and tell her what a pleasure it was. I had already set up a new phone number because I knew she was getting close. I could see through the cracks I hadn't meant to leave open. I'd planned the 'I love you' line a week in advance—figured it'd get her legs open, and it did.

What I didn't plan for was how sick I felt saying it.

I almost convinced myself to walk away that night; a better man would have done just that. But the allure was just too tempting to resist.

I was obsessed. Had to have her. Had to know what she felt like. Had to know whether she'd crack or if I could perform well enough to keep her calm, let me in without a flicker of fear. Turns out I deserved a fucking Oscar—she trusted me completely. No anxiety, no panic. She let me take her without hesitation.

I could have easily taken advantage of her when she was drunk that night, but I convinced myself that would be cheating. I pushed aside the truth that I wanted to draw out my time with her, that I wasn't ready for it to end. Admitting love for her felt like cheating too, but the words just tumbled out before I could stop them. I had rehearsed it in my mind, but in that instant, it felt real, and I knew I had to face the inevitable conclusion. I couldn't let myself continue to feel any longer.

I thought I would snap back to reality the moment I stepped outside, but here I am, nine agonising days later, obsessively checking her emails like a lovesick teenager who just got his first blow job.

Each message is becoming more painful to read, yet I've managed to hold it together so far. Reading her apparent loneliness again hits me like a physical blow, as if someone had sliced me open.

I anticipated her anger, I was willing to risk it, thinking that a mix of denial and humour might lighten the mood, clearly that's not the case. I broke her. Lost her. And instead of stepping back, like any sane person would, I keep pulling her deeper—because even now, knowing what I've done, I can't let go. I think this is guilt. Or maybe just the psychopaths version of it.

If nothing else, I hope our brief exchanges will prompt her to reach out to Jeanie, giving me just a sliver of her presence that I know I don't deserve.

She's likely never going to grasp what truly went wrong. She's drowning in self-blame, but only because I made sure she never saw the full picture. She never stood a chance against the illusion I built.

I was the ideal guy in her eyes, but in reality, I'm just the type of person she believes all men are.

Instead of fucking her body without her consent, I fucked with her head. And that might be more damaging.

It's ironic, because she's definitely fucking with my head too. I've never felt this way about anyone before. Just saying that feels so foreign to me.

How do people even deal with all these emotions? It's a miracle we don't descend into chaos, especially since right now, I feel like I could set the world ablaze just to hear her voice again.

I've gone a little unhinged. But I'm fixated. Obsessed.

I *will* find a way to see her again.

CHAPTER 4

ALLY

Just when I thought I was finally clawing my way back to some version of normal, he sends that message—yanking me straight back into the chaos. My mind feels even more tangled than it did the morning I woke up to find him gone.

Why now? Why was yesterday special?

What kind of person swings from warmth to cold like

that, without warning?

I sit on the couch, laptop open but ignored. *The Life and Times of the Cat Hair Knitter* stares back at me from the screen, unread and completely abandoned. My thoughts are consumed by one thing—Jax Beckett. The enigma. The storm I keep stepping into, even when I know better.

Hours slip by. I lose track of time, stuck in the spiral of what-if's and why's, until frustration becomes a physical ache.

Jeanie warned me: *You might never understand him.*

So, here I am, 2:30 on a Thursday afternoon, sipping a tequila sunrise and stewing over the maddening nature of men.

The buzz of the intercom jolts me. I blink, drag myself off the couch, and press the button.

"Hey, Paul."

"Miss Barlow, there's a delivery for you."

I haven't ordered anything. Probably Tyler again, trying to cheer me up with another pair of shoes. He took the breakup harder than I did, in some ways. He still wants to punch Jax in the face, but admitted he was glad I'd had someone—someone safe—who made me feel something, that didn't require me kissing a hundred frogs. That thought just twists the knife.

"Thanks, Paul. Send it up."

There's a knock a few minutes later. I open the door expecting cardboard and bubble wrap—but instead, I forget how to breathe.

A stunning bouquet of about two dozen red roses in a glass vase overwhelms my senses; they're not just beautiful but also emit a fragrance that's simply intoxicating. Yet, what truly leaves me speechless is the sight of the man holding them.

He looks different. Older. Shadows under his eyes, rough stubble giving him a more rugged edge—but it's the way he holds himself, slightly slouched, worn down, that truly stops me.

Even so, he's still painfully handsome. His honey-coloured eyes meet mine, and for a moment I'm frozen, caught in some gravitational pull I thought I'd broken free from.

"Ally," he says quietly, like he's not sure he has the right to say my name.

I step forward before I even realise I'm moving, drawn to him like always.

And then it hits me—sadness, confusion, fury—all at once. Fury rises to the top.

I take the vase from his hands.

He lets go.

So do I.

It crashes to the floor, a violent explosion of shattering glass and splashing water.

I don't wait. I turn, and slam the door behind me.

"Ally, wait!" he calls out, pounding on the door. "I'm not leaving until you talk to me!"

I press my forehead to the cool wood. My hands shake. I don't know what to say, don't even know if I want to say anything.

More pounding. Then—did he just kick the door? "HANNAH!"

My eyes snap open.

What the actual fuck?

I grip the handle and yank the door open so hard it rattles in the frame.

"Wow. That actually works," he says, smirking.

"What the fuck is wrong with you?" I snap, fury bubbling up fast now.

"It gets your attention when your brother says it. Figured I'd try," he says, casually, like this is all some joke.

I move to slam the door again, but his hand catches it.

"I'm sorry, okay? I'm really fucking sorry," he says, voice softer now. Less bravado. More wreckage.

"Why, Jax? *Why*?" My frustration spills over into something raw.

"I can't tell you. But I know I fucked up. And I miss you."

He pushes the door open wider and steps over the mess, closing the distance between us like none of it matters. His hands grip my hips, pulling me into him— and then he kisses me.

It's not sweet.

It's not gentle.

It's *desperate*.

A kiss like survival. Like he's starving for me. His hands dig into my sides, hard enough to bruise. His mouth crashes into mine with an urgency that steals the air from my lungs.

I respond in kind before I can think. Getting lost in the feel of him, the smell of him—the heat, the ache, the memory of everything we shared.

Then the illusion breaks. Just like we did.

I break away. His forehead rests against mine, his hands shifting to cradle my face, breath hot and fast.

Then I lift my knee.

Hard.

He drops like a stone, groaning as he hits the floor.

"You can see yourself out," I say, voice ice-cold, as I turn and walk away. My bedroom door slams behind me like a full stop.

If Jax Beckett taught me anything, it's this: I know how to stand up for myself against unwanted affection. Even if it takes me a moment too long.

CHAPTER 5

JAX

She's pissed. More than pissed. Nuclear. I knew she'd be angry, but I didn't think she'd go full Mortal Kombat and try to neuter me. Ollie warned me. Said she'd rip me a new one. But I didn't think she could hurt me. Not like *that*.

And not just the knee to the groin—the look in her

eyes.

That was the real weapon.

I should've seen it coming. Disappearing after the best night of her life—after I made her feel things no one else ever could. That's on me. I miscalculated. I thought she'd be confused. Maybe hurt. But not like this.

Maybe I waited too long. Ten days was pushing it. But I needed space. Not from her—from myself. I needed to cool the voices, sort through the mess in my head. I tried deleting her number, wiping our photos, cutting every tie. But I still knew the smell of her vanilla shampoo. Still tracked the timestamp of her last email. I watched her through the cameras at her building, counted how many steps it took her to get from her building to the café she always goes to.

Thirty-two.

I memorised it. Just like I memorised the way her lips part when she reads something funny on her phone. Or the way she always looks over her shoulder before unlocking her door.

I tell myself I'm just… keeping her safe.

Flawed

So yeah. Maybe I'm not the hero of this story.

But I never claimed to be.

She's *mine*.

Whether she admits it or not.

So here I am. Sitting on her couch like I belong here. Like I didn't ghost her. Like I didn't vanish without a word. She doesn't know I've been in her apartment before today—while she was at the supermarket. Just once. I didn't take anything. Didn't touch anything.

Just… stood in her bedroom, breathing her in.

Pathetic? Maybe.

But I needed to know she was real. That I hadn't made her up. Because sometimes it feels that way.

ABCDEFU blares from her room on loop. Every time it restarts, it's like a punishment I deserve. Twenty minutes later, she finally turns it off.

I hear her door open, and when I see her, I forget how to breathe.

She looks broken. And somehow even more beautiful because of it.

Her eyes are puffy. Red. Her lip trembling like she's trying not to cry again.

Good. Let her hurt. Because I do.

I stand without thinking and go to her. Wrap my arms around her like they never should've let go. Her body melts against mine, and I almost groan from the relief of it.

"I'm sorry," I whisper hoarsely.

She doesn't push me away. Instead, she cries.

Her tears soak through my shirt, but I don't move. I hold her tighter. Stroke her back. Kiss the top of her head like that'll erase everything.

"I'm sorry," I say again.

This isn't guilt. Not really. It's more like frustration—at myself, for not keeping her when I had her. At her, for not understanding what I am.

I was trying to protect her. From me. From the darkness. From the things I've done.

But maybe that was a mistake.

"Tell me why," she says quietly.

"I can't."

"Why not?"

"Because once you know, you'll never look at me the same again."

And I need her to keep looking at me like I'm not a monster. Even if I have to burn everything else down to keep that gaze.

She lifts her face. Tear-streaked. Wrecked. Perfect.

I brush her cheek.

"You should go," she says. But her body doesn't move. She doesn't mean it.

"I can't," I reply. "I won't."

She stiffens. That fire returns to her eyes, and I know she's about to lash out again. My hands twitch toward my crotch instinctively.

"You planning to knee me again?" I ask, more amused than afraid.

"I haven't decided."

A silent moment passes before she speaks again.

"You've got two choices, Jax," she says, steel laces her words. "Explain. Or walk away."

There's a third option, of course.

The one where I never leave.

Where I keep coming back until she forgets she ever hated me. Until I'm the only one she trusts. The only one who knows her. Until her resistance breaks like the glass in the hallway.

"I'm trying," I say, softer now. "I'm trying to be the version of me you don't have to be afraid of."

She laughs. Bitter. Hollow. "That version doesn't exist."

She's wrong. It does. It can.

He exists when she's around.

I lean in, kiss her forehead again. My lips linger. She exhales, shaky and her eyes close. Her defences falter.

That's all I need.

"Can't you just accept that I fucked up?" My voice is low, intimate.

She opens her eyes. Cold now. Distant.

She's slipping away again.

So I step back. Give her space.

Let her think she has control. It's the trick to all of this—*letting them think they're choosing you.*

I head to the door. I don't look back.

But I know she's watching me. I can feel her eyes, like heat on the back of my neck.

Good.

Let her wonder where I'm going.

Flawed

Let her miss me.

Because I'll be back. Tomorrow. Or the next day. Or the day after that.

She's not done with me. Not even close.

Even if I have to break her down, piece by piece, until there's nothing left but the version of her that belongs to me.

CHAPTER 6

ALLY

I barely slept last night—landed in that weird, restless limbo where your body feels dead but your brain won't shut up.

Everything aches. My limbs feel heavy, my chest too tight. The exhaustion is bone-deep, but the thoughts wouldn't stop. Just kept circling back to that fucking conversation. Over and over.

My body reacted to him. I let him kiss me. Let myself lean into him, and then completely lost it—sobbing like some shattered thing against his chest.

And now I'm stuck here, trapped between instinct and logic. Because my mind keeps screaming no, but everything else whispers *maybe*.

Trust? That's not something I give easily. Not after… *No. Don't go there.*

But the truth is, at that moment, I felt safe. Like actually safe. And that? That's rarer than gold.

I need air. Space. Coffee. Anything to shake this fog.

Outside, the morning is already too bright. I give Paul a quick wave but don't stop to chat—I can't. I feel… brittle. Like one wrong word and I'll crack wide open.

I slip into the short line at the café, dragging in shallow breaths. My thoughts loop back again. Same phrases. Same confusion.

I can't do that. You'll never look at me the same way again.

What does that even mean?

Would it be worse if he had no excuse? Or is it more

terrifying that he does—but won't say it out loud?

The unknown is eating me alive. My brain already fills in the blanks with the worst-case scenarios.

Maybe he's a killer?

Ridiculous.

Still a fuckboy?

Possible.

Sociopath?

I actually snort at that one. He's too warm. Too thoughtful. Still a manipulative prick, but not *that* kind.

Ugh. Just—fuck this confusion.

"Ally?"

"Shit, sorry, I zoned out. Just the usual, thanks, Claire."

Claire grins, clearly fighting laughter. She's all sunshine—blonde ponytail, bright blue eyes, pink bow. Probably too perky for this early in the day, but she means well.

"What's funny?"

She shakes her head. "It's already sorted."

"What is?"

"Your coffee. And food. Paid up for a while."

I blink. "By who?"

"Guy named Sam called and set you up with an account."

"I don't know anyone named Sam."

"Said he's a fireman. Honey-coloured eyes. And—" she pauses, absolutely losing it— "lickable abs."

I groan, covering my face. "Are you kidding me?"

"Dead serious," she wheezes between giggles.

"Who even talks like that?" I groan more to myself than her.

"Apparently you, after a few shots."

Heat rushes to my face.

"So, he's paid for my order?"

"Yep. Set up a tab and said he'll top it up next week."

"Is that right?"

Cheeky fucker! Two can play at his game.

As I step out of the coffee shop, juggling three bags packed with nearly $100 worth of food, guilt hits fast—like I've gone overboard, reckless and wasteful.

Wanting the gesture to mean something, I walk the three blocks to the nearby park. He's there—same spot, sitting on the edge of a bench with a weathered backpack at his feet.

"Hey," I say, holding out the bags. "Thought you might be hungry."

He looks up, eyes crinkling. "You're not wrong." He takes the food carefully, like it might vanish. "Name's Will."

"Nice to meet you, Will." I sit beside him. "There's enough in there for a few people."

"Good," he says. "I've got mates nearby. They'll be stoked." He pauses, then adds, "People don't usually stop. Let alone bring pastries."

I laugh lightly. "They're good ones too. From a café that thinks it's too fancy for takeaway boxes."

That earns a chuckle. We sit for a while, talking about nothing and everything. When I finally ask, "Mind if I grab a photo?" he shrugs, still smiling.

"Go ahead. Just make sure I look handsome."

There's a gentleness in his eyes, the kind that feels rare lately. As I leave, I feel lighter—not fixed, not absolved, but steadier somehow.

It's the first time in a while something has felt good for the right reasons and I know I'll be back.

I text Jax the photo—Will holding the bags, the coffee shop logo clearly visible. A simple image, but it says enough.

Ally: Well played, Sam!

His reply comes almost instantly

Jax: Touché.

◆ ◆ ◆

As the afternoon drags on, I find myself back on the couch, I stare at the half-finished cat knitting project like it personally insulted me. I need a distraction. Something darker that's more fitting for the mess in my head.

I open my freelance profile but as soon as I do, *The Bitch Song* starts blaring.

"This daily check-in is getting old," I mutter.

"Hello to you too. Don't be such a bitch—it doesn't suit you."

"Oh please, the new me owns the bitch vibe, thank you very much."

"New you? How many personalities are you juggling in that skull?"

"Just enough to keep you guessing."

"You call the cop back yet?"

I pause. "Nope. Not in the mood for that particular disaster."

"Take your time. No pressure."

"I will. Just… not today."

"You alright, Ally?"

I hesitate. He deserves honesty, but I can't find the words.

Ty's really been making an effort. Two straight weeks and he hasn't slipped up calling me anything but Ally. After twenty years of another name, it can't be easy for him and I appreciate that.

"I'm fine, just like yesterday." I lie. "You don't have to check in every day."

"I've been there Ally, I know how bad heartbreak sucks arse! It feels like someone has ripped open your chest and is squeezing your soul so tightly that it might consume you — like there's no way out."

Ty doesn't talk about her much, but when he does,

when Natalie slips into the conversation, I feel that familiar sting of guilt. She was the one girl he really loved. Poured everything he had into that relationship. But in the end, it just wasn't enough.

They tried, God knows they tried. But he was drowning—trying to hold me together while quietly falling apart himself. No matter how many times I told him I had nothing but love for Nat, it didn't change what it did to him.

It all got too heavy, too hard. They let go. And even though he'll never say it, I know he still carries the weight of it. Since then, his weekends have blurred into a carousel of blondes and brunettes. Never a redhead. I think that part still hurts too much.

"Ty—"

"Don't," he says, his voice cracking.

The guilt hits me all over again, heavy and familiar. Desperate to shift the mood, I blurt out the first thing that comes to mind—the homeless man I met today.

I brace myself for the lecture, already glancing back at my laptop. This is going to take a while.

Just as I refocus on the screen, a new job listing pops

up.

Sam the Fireman.

What the actual fuck?

I click the link, blinking at the words:

Meet Sam, the stupid fireman who fucks up royally and gets kneed in the balls. Spoiler alert—he probably deserved it.

Draft count: 21 words

Reading time: 1 minute

Job would suit: Specific person. Don't apply—you'd know if it's you.

Writing style: Terrible

About the author: Miserable, with sore balls.

I push aside the wave of emotions the ad stirs up and return to the main page—only to find the same listing posted over and over. The entire first page is just variations of this ridiculous cry for attention.

Frustrated, I slam my laptop shut with more force than necessary and toss it onto the couch beside me.

I rush Tyler off the phone and press my palms to my eyes, trying to breathe through the spiral.

My hands are shaking. Everything feels too much

again. Too loud. Too raw.

I reach for my phone, ignoring the tremor in my fingers because it's time to call the cop back.

My mood can't get any worse so might as well get this shit show over with.

CHAPTER 7

JAX

It's Friday afternoon, and I've finally wrapped up my work for the week, which means I have no excuse not to sit alone and enjoy my good friend —bourbon—straight from the bottle. Just as I'm starting to get into the groove, enjoying the quiet, the doorbell rings.

I groan. Loudly.

Flawed

I just want to be left the fuck alone.

But I figure it's probably less hassle to answer the door than to deal with the aftermath of another broken window, so I drag myself off the couch. When I open it, I'm met with Ollie's beaming smile and two bottles of bourbon—one in each hand.

"Howdy, little brother! I come bearing gifts."

"The only reason I'm not slamming the door in your annoyingly cheerful face is because of those bottles."

I plop back down on the couch, take another swig from my own bottle, while Ollie lingers, clearly hesitating.

"Seriously, Jax, you need to stop this," he finally says.

"Why?" I ask, genuinely not seeing the problem.

"Because it's not healthy. And it's not like you. Have you even been to the gym lately?"

I roll my eyes and throw back, "Fuck that guy, he sucks. I'm Sam now."

Ollie blinks. "Who the fuck is Sam?"

"He's a fireman. He's pretty awesome." I feel a flicker of pride. My little freelance troll project is honestly the most fun I've had in days.

"What the actual fuck are you talking about? How much have you had to drink?"

I'm about to answer his dumbass question when a loud bang on the door interrupts me. I groan again and rub my temples, silently begging the universe to just let me suffer in peace.

When I make no move, Ollie strides over and opens the door.

And then, like a hurricane, she storms in.

"Ally?" I say, caught somewhere between confusion and that stupid thrill I can't ever seem to shake when she's near.

"WHAT THE ACTUAL FUCK IS WRONG WITH YOU? HAVE YOU COMPLETELY LOST YOUR FUCKING MIND?"

Okay. So maybe she didn't find the job ad as hilarious as I did.

"Well, hello to you too, beautiful."

She's vibrating with rage. "Seriously, Jax? You think this is a joke? It's not funny! You think that knee to the balls hurt? Just wait. You haven't felt anything yet."

"What happened to the sweet, shy girl I fell for? Is she here? I'd much rather talk to her. She's a lot nicer."

Total lie. Ally, all fired up and shouting at me like this? It's the first time my cock has stirred in almost two weeks. She's fucking hot when she's angry.

"She's comfortable enough with you to shove her foot up your ass. This is serious, Jax! I saw you yesterday—how could you not tell me he's pressing charges against you? You could be in serious trouble because of me. The police officer I spoke to said you're not even taking this seriously. You laughed at him!"

She's yelling, pacing, and I'm just watching her—almost amused.

Honestly, I didn't think she'd get this worked up.

"Wait, *that's* why you're losing your shit? Ally, I don't care that he's pressing assault charges. If he were standing in front of me right now, I'd hit him again without a second thought."

And isn't that the *tame* version.

Given another shot, I'd peel his skin off, strip by strip, and make him watch every second of it.

I wouldn't stop—

Not when he screamed.

Not when he begged.

Especially not then.

"What the fuck?" Ollie again, his tone sharp with concern. Right. Forgot he was even here.

"And I appreciate the thought," Ally says, her voice shifting, a little softer but still pissed. "But how could you not tell me? I had to come all the way over here."

"You could've just called if you were going to yell at me," I mutter, a little defensive now.

She snaps, "I deleted your number!"

Oof.

That one lands, hook line and sinker, to the chest. The excitement I felt seeing her drops right out of me.

I sigh before I can stop myself. "I had more important things on my mind when I saw you. But you're right. We should talk about this over dinner."

She eyes me, hard. "Are you going to explain why you left?"

"I can't do that."

She snatches the bottle from my hand, takes a massive swig, then shoves it back against my chest.

"If you can't tell me, then I don't want to see you. And spoiler alert—Sam definitely deserved it!"

Then she spins and storms out, and I'm left sitting there with the first real grin I've worn in weeks. That girl is fire.

But the smile fades when I catch Ollie glaring at me. It could cut steel.

"Don't even start," I snap.

"Someone's pressing charges against you?"

"Yep," I reply casually, as if it's not a big deal.

"What the fuck did you do this time?" he presses, knowing this isn't my first brush with the law. Usually, it's smaller offences like trespassing, pub fights, vandalism and that unfortunate misunderstanding involving solicitation- selling, not buying, of course.

I give him the rundown—the pub, the broken jaw, the visit to Ally's place, the knee to the nuts. His face shifts the further I get, from disbelief to reluctant understanding. He even chuckles when I get to the part where I dropped to my knees like a sack of shit, agreeing that I deserved it.

Then he asks the inevitable.

"Why not just tell her?"

"And say what? Hey, Ally, how was your day? By the way, you know those warm, fuzzy feelings normal people have? Yeah—I'm missing that gene completely."

"You're not a psychopath, Jackson."

Ugh. Full name. Dad voice. I shoot my best *really?* look.

But he's not wrong. Not entirely. Technically I am undiagnosed.

But what am I supposed to say? *Hey, Ally, I meant every kiss, but I never felt them the way you did. All that soft stuff—love, guilt, compassion—it doesn't come naturally to me. It never has.*

I'm just wired wrong. Always have been.

People think emotions are some kind of moral compass. Like if you don't feel what they feel, you must be flawed. Dangerous. Less human. And maybe they're right. But I've survived like this for years—observing, mimicking, giving people the version of me they want. It's second nature by now. Just not with her.

With Ally, the lines blurred and I started slipping. Showing too much. Wanting more than I should. And now that she knows I'm not what I pretended to be... what the hell do I have left?

"Just tell her. What do you have to lose? She won't see you otherwise," Ollie adds helpfully.

She already doesn't see me. Not really. Not the real me, the version I kept hidden.

But maybe that's the point. Maybe if I peel it back— strip away the charm, the rehearsed lines, the palatable version of me—and show her the truth, ugly and unfiltered, sharp edges and all... she'll finally stop searching for something in me that was never there.

Maybe then she'll stop blaming herself.

I won't get to keep her—not like this. But if I can ease even a fraction of her pain, give her something real to hold onto instead of the hollow fantasy I fed her... maybe that'll be enough.

Just enough to let her go.

I pull out my phone and type out a message before I can talk myself out of it.

Jax: Have dinner with me and I'll explain.

Ally: I'm free Sunday night.

Jax: I'll pick you up at 7.

Ally: No, just tell me where to meet you. And leave fireman Sam at home!

Well fuck.

This is going to be an interesting dinner.

CHAPTER 8

ALLY

I spend half of Saturday morning hyping myself up like I'm heading into battle. If I can just convince Ty I'm okay, maybe he'll finally ease up on the daily check-ins and relentless calls. It drives me mental how much he worries—and the guilt eats at me, knowing it's all because I'm still wrecked over Jax.

Just as I'm shoving the vacuum back into the closet,

laughter floats in from outside. Great, Ty brought Nate. Because of course, what I really need today is a goddamn intervention.

The front door swings open and Ty strolls in like he owns the place, dropping a slab of beer on the counter. He gives me a once-over.

"You look good," he says, like it genuinely surprises him.

I cross my arms. "I keep telling you I'm fine."

Nate appears beside me, wrapping his arms around me before I can dodge it. "So you should be. He's a dick anyway."

My spine goes rigid. Heat flares in my chest—defensive, instant, and completely irrational. "He's not a dick," I snap, harsher than I mean to.

Nate doesn't flinch. "He definitely is."

"You don't even know him!" The words tear out of me before I can stop them.

"Why are you so worked up?"

"I'm not worked up!" Total lie. And we both know it. "I just don't get why you think he's a dick. I thought you liked him."

"There is something very off about him," Nate says, too casually, like he's testing how far he can push before I crack.

I open my mouth, then close it. I don't even know why I'm defending Jax. Not after everything. After what he put me through. But I am—and that confuses me more than anything. It's like my brain hasn't caught up to the part where I'm supposed to be done with him.

I glance at Ty for backup. Nothing. He's just standing there, arms crossed, gaze drifting. Coward.

"There's nothing *off* about him," I say through clenched teeth. "He's perfect."

And of course, Ty chooses now to speak, "If he's so perfect, why aren't you seeing him anymore?"

"I am." Shit. "I mean—I'm not *seeing* him. Not like that. But I'm seeing him tomorrow night. For dinner."

Ty's brow furrows. Nate looks like he's watching a car crash in slow motion.

"Are you sure that's a good idea?" Ty asks gently.

Nate adds, not so gently, "That's a terrible idea. It's just a booty call."

"Watch it," Ty snaps, but I'm already on the defence.

"It's not a booty call!"

Nate scoffs. "Come on, Ally. It's a last-ditch effort to get in your pants. I know how guys think."

My words catch in my throat. I want to explain that it's not like that, but I don't even know what *it* is. Instead, I deflect.

"Michael's pressing assault charges against him," I blurt. "We're meeting to talk about it."

Nate's expression softens. "Shit. I didn't know."

But Ty doesn't even blink. His face is a blank slate.

"You knew?" I ask, low and tight.

He sighs. "Nat told me. She was trying to talk Michael out of it before you found out."

I stare at him. "When the hell did you talk to Nat?"

He shrugs, avoiding my eyes. "We chat sometimes."

"And you didn't tell me?" I snap.

"I didn't want to make things worse."

I throw my hands up. "Jesus, Ty! You can't keep things like this from me! I lost it when the cop told me. I went straight to Jax's and threatened to shove my foot up his arse!"

Nate snorts, and I shoot him a glare.

"I mean it! You both need to stop trying to protect me. Is there anything else I should know?"

Ty flicks his eyes to the ceiling. "Nothing else. Let's just move on, yeah? I'll grab the drinks. You set up the PlayStation."

The rest of the afternoon drags under a weird, heavy silence. No one mentions Jax or Michael again. Ty is unusually quiet, and his sarcasm has gone AWOL. Nate fills the gaps with banter, but it's not enough to shake the unease coiling in my gut.

◆ ◆ ◆

Last night, I downed a bottle of wine and chased it with a few tequila shots—desperate to black out before my brain could spiral. It worked… for a while.

But the second I opened my eyes this morning, the dread came crashing back. Heavier than before.

I fire off an email to Jeanie. No pleasantries, no filter, just a brain dump. I don't even ask for advice. I just need it out of me. There's too much tangled up in Jax's name alone. The good parts—the laughter, the way he used to look at me like I was the only person in the room, like I actually mattered.

And then there's the other side. The vanishing act. The man who shattered me and didn't even blink.

I feel like I'm being pulled in two directions—part of me still tethered to him, the other screaming to cut loose and run. My heart and my head are stuck in a constant tug-of-war, and I'm so fucking tired of it.

At noon, my phone pings.

Jax: What's more influential? Your brain or your heart?

I freeze. The timing is too perfect. He does this sometimes. Drops these questions that cut straight through me, like he's wired into my thoughts.

It's unsettling how often it happens. So precise, it feels less like coincidence and more like he's reading a script I didn't know I wrote.

It's… unnerving. Like he's inside my head, feeding off my doubts, amplifying my confusion. The kind of unsettling that makes me want to respond, but I can't tell if he's asking out of genuine curiosity or if he's just playing mind games.

And then the thought hits me: What if he *does* know? What if he sees straight through me, sees exactly how torn I am, and he's pulling these strings on purpose, knowing he's got me wrapped around his finger?

The idea twists in my gut.

I stare at the message, hesitating, caught in the whirlwind of my own thoughts, unsure if I'm overthinking or if it's exactly what I should expect from someone like him. And the worst part—the part I can't admit out loud—is that I don't know how to stop.

◆ ◆ ◆

Okay, deep breaths. I stare at the warzone that is my bedroom. After trying on half my wardrobe, I finally settle on something that screams *I'm fine and definitely not trying too hard*: a knee-length pink denim skirt, fitted white top, silver glitter sneakers and pearl string hairband, because you're never fully dressed without a hair accessory. Not sexy. Not sweet. Just… me. And that has to be enough tonight.

Jeanie called not long ago and pushed me to give him a fair shot. *What if there's a reason for all of it?* she had said. *Closure can be unpredictable, and you never really know how it will come about.*

If tonight goes sideways, I'm at least hoping to draw some understanding from the wreckage.

I just want clarity. Anything but the limbo that has been choking the life out of me.

Jax texted to meet at the bar where we first had drinks. I can't tell if that's romantic or just another way to twist the knife.

The walk there feels like a death march, each step squeezing my chest tighter. I spot him instantly—leaning against the wall, hair tousled, leg bouncing with tense energy.

Jax Beckett, nervous?

He straightens the second he sees me. Eyes lock on mine, sharp and electric. Like I'm his gravity.

I stop a mere breath away. He smells like sandalwood and sin, and my knees nearly give out. No anger this time, just the ache of missing him, raw and dangerous.

He brushes a thumb across my cheek. "I missed you, beautiful."

I step back, clearing my throat. "We should go in. I

could really use a drink."

"I'm turning you into an alcoholic," he mutters, half a joke, half a warning.

Inside, it's just as I remember—open space, quiet corners—but it feels different. The air is thick with unspoken tension.

Jax leads me to a booth in the back and disappears to the bar, returning with a bottle of Gembrook Hill and four tequila shots.

"One each for now, one for later. You'll need it," he says.

His tone isn't cruel. But it's not warm, either.

I knock back the shot and brace myself.

After a long beat, I ask, "I've never seen you nervous before. Is it really that bad?"

He runs a hand through his hair, his leg bouncing until he catches it and forces himself still.

"I've been rehearsing this for the past day and a half," he says. "It's harder out loud."

I wait.

"This started off different for me," he adds, eyes not quite meeting mine. "Different than it did for you."

I stiffen. "Different how?"

His gaze lifts, locking onto mine. "What drew you to me, Ally?"

Thrown, I blink. "I… felt safe. With you."

He almost smiles—almost. "You were never safe with me. Not at first."

A chill creeps down my spine. "What the hell does that even mean?"

He takes a breath, like he's about to dive underwater. "I don't experience emotions the way you do. Empathy, guilt, remorse—they don't come naturally to me."

A stunned laugh escapes before I can control it. I honestly didn't think he'd give me a straight answer, but this is just absurd. There's no way he expects me to buy this crap, right?

"If you're going to lie, at least make it believable."

He flinches, then takes my hand, tentative.

"I'm sorry, beautiful. I wish I was lying. You called me perfect… but that was just me *acting* perfect. Every move I made—the way I listened, what I said, how I touched you—was calculated. Based on what you needed at the time. Me responding to what you wanted in those moments."

My throat tightens. "You were *kind*. You understood me."

"Because I studied you. I mirrored what you needed. You created the perfect scenarios to form connections."

My voice cracks, "Why go through all that effort?"

Something in his face shifts. A shadow, cold and clinical. And I *know* the answer before he says it.

"You were a puzzle," he says. "That night, I saw something fragile in you. I wanted to know how many moves it would take to make you fall."

My stomach lurches. "What it would take to fuck me? That's why you left? Because the game was over?" I shove my stool back. "I think I'm going to be sick!"

"It started that way," he admits quietly. "But then… it didn't stay that way."

I take a step back, distancing myself from him. My body vibrates—rage, heartbreak, shame all tangled into something unholy. "So everything was fake? Every kiss, every word?"

"Not fake. Chosen." He is calm, almost soothing. "I chose to do those things. That choice was real. The why behind it… is complicated. I don't necessarily feel emotions the way you do, but I can appreciate them. I can understand their value. I can be good to you, Ally. Maybe even better than someone driven by messy, unpredictable emotions."

I stare at him, horrified. "You want me to love a fake version of you you invented?"

His eyes shine with something close to desperation. "He doesn't have to be fake. I can *be* him, if that's what you want."

My hands tremble. "You're a fucking monster," I whisper, voice breaking. "You let me fall for a lie."

"He doesn't have to be a lie," he insists, leaning forward like proximity will convince me. "I can turn it on anytime."

"I don't even know who you are. You decided to play god with my emotions and the worst part? The guy I fell for isn't even real; he's just an act."

"I can be him whenever you need. You just have to tell me what you want, and I'll make it happen for you. You need to understand, Ally, I don't feel emotions, but with you, I feel everything."

Has he completely lost his mind? There's no way he thinks I'd want to be with a fake version of him. My heart wants to scream at him 'yes, just be that guy'. We can live happily ever after and ride into the sunset and live in the land of make-believe and fairytales. But my head… my head knows it's wrong to want him to be something that he's not, just for my sake.

My heart lurches, traitorous. But my brain screams louder.

I reach for the last two shots and knock them back, one after the other. The burn in my throat has nothing on the fire ripping through my chest.

"You broke me," I whisper. "And I let you."

Then I'm on my feet, bag in hand, moving before I can second-guess it.

Closure?

Closure can kiss my arse!

CHAPTER 9

JAX

I catch up to her just as she steps onto the street, but I don't call out. I don't touch her. I want to —god, I *need* to—but I hang back, watching her storm off like I'm already a ghost.

Maybe Ollie was right. Maybe the truth matters, but it doesn't make this feel any less like bleeding out slowly.

Flawed

The truth was a grenade and I pulled the damn pin.

When she finally stops outside her building, she turns —eyes still blazing, like she could set me on fire just by looking at me. But there's something else there too. A flicker of hesitation. A crack in her armour.

Before I can say another word—another pathetic apology she'll never believe—I close the distance between us and kiss her.

It's reckless. Desperate. A last-ditch attempt to tether her to me before she slips away for good.

To my surprise, she kisses me back—hard. Her fury fuels it, her lips crashing against mine with enough heat to burn. My hands grip her hips as if anchoring myself to the only thing in this world that's ever made me feel real. Her tongue tangles with mine, frantic and furious, and it knocks the breath out of me. I barely notice the sting when she bites my lip, the metallic taste of blood grounds me in the chaos.

One hand fists in my hair, the other pushes at my chest, as if she doesn't know whether to pull me closer or shove me away.

When we finally break apart, she leans in again, like

her body is still fighting her mind. Our foreheads press together, her chest rising and falling in sharp breaths. My hands won't leave her hips. I can't let go. If I do, I'm afraid she'll disappear.

Her eyes open slowly. There's confusion swirling in them. Hurt. Need.

She slips her hand into mine and tugs me forward.

We move in silence. The elevator ride is wordless, every second stretches with unbearable weight. My heart hammers like a warning, like a countdown. I don't know what I'm walking into. I don't know if this is forgiveness or a goodbye dressed in lust.

The moment we step into her apartment, she's on me again. Her fingers grab the front of my shirt, pulling me down to her mouth, and her kiss is brutal. Her teeth sink into my lip again and it hurts—but I welcome the pain. It's better than the emptiness that's been eating me alive since the second I left her.

She shoves me against the wall—*that* wall. The same one where I pinned her during her panic attack. The irony is not lost on me because now I feel like I'm on the verge of falling apart.

I kiss her back like I'm dying. Because maybe I am.

She tears off my shirt like it's nothing. Her nails scrape my chest and I hiss, grabbing a handful of her hair and pulling her tighter. I want to slow this down, to savour her, but she's grinding against me and I'm close to losing all sense of control. Then she reaches for my belt—

And I freeze.

I grab her wrists, halting her. My breath is ragged, my thoughts spinning. This is all I've wanted for weeks, and I'm the one stopping it?

Her eyes widen, lips parted and cheeks flushed.

"Don't turn into a good guy on me now," she whispers, voice thick with frustration and something else—something broken.

I'm shaking. I want to do this right. I want to be better. But she's not asking for that. She's asking for me —the version capable of setting the world on fire, and she's handing me the goddamn match.

Fuck it. Old habits don't just die hard, they come back louder.

I grab her waist and pull her against me again. This

time, my kiss is different—slow, coaxing, deceptive. I don't want to be, but I need her to think. To feel.

She jumps up, legs wrapping around me like instinct, and I carry her to the bedroom. She's hungry, trying to take over the kiss, but I ease up, trying—failing—to be the kind of man who doesn't just take. I want her to see I can be like Sam—safe. Stable. But her eyes… she's looking at me like she doesn't recognise me. And that stings worse than anything else.

I brush her cheek. Kiss her slowly. Gentle.

"Fuck me like the real you," she breathes against my lips, and something inside me snaps.

She wants the real me. The unfiltered, selfish, possessive bastard I've spent years learning to cage.

I kiss her like I'm starving. My hands are everywhere, greedy and rough. Her clothes come off in pieces. Her panties, I rip them like they are in my way. Everything that separates us is in the way.

Her scent floods me. Her heat scrambles my brain. I want to hesitate. I expect resistance. But she arches into me, moaning when I bite her, her nails raking fire down my back.

I shed my pants fast and return to her, but she's already taking control, dragging me down by the neck. Her heels dig into my arse as she grinds into me, but I hesitate. That damn voice in my head—the one she put there—screams at me to slow down, to think—but I don't. I *can't*.

I slide into her, and her gasp splits the air. I stop, waiting, heart slamming into my ribs like it's trying to escape.

"Are you okay?" my voice cracks. Please be okay.

"Don't talk," she growls.

And, fuck me, I listen.

I start to move, one hand buried in her hair, the other gripping her hip like a lifeline. The rhythm is fast, raw, unhinged. I'm fucking her like I want to burn us both alive. This isn't making love. This is a war cry. A claim. A fucking confession. I know this will either fix us or destroy us, but either way I've already lost my grip on my restraint.

She tenses beneath me, and I want to stop—I should stop—but her legs lock around me tighter, holding me in. Begging me silently not to go.

I flip her, grab her hips, and slide back into her with a groan so guttural it's barely human. I spank her, sharp and quick, and she doesn't protest, just moans louder.

I pull her upright by her hair, flush to my chest, and find her clit with my fingers, trying to balance the pain with pleasure. She wasn't ready to be fucked like this—not physically, not emotionally—but she's soaked, gripping me tight, and she's fucking loving it.

Her body trembles.

Her breath catches.

And when I whisper against the shell of her ear—"Be a good girl for me, Ally. Come all over my cock while I fuck you like a whore—"she shatters.

Her body convulses, a silent scream frozen on her lips. She falls back against me, limp and wrecked, and I wrap my arms around her like I can keep her safe from the world—when I'm the one she needs saving from.

I kiss her shoulder. I breathe her in.

"Are you alright, beautiful?"

Because if I've hurt her—really hurt her—I'll never come back from it.

She tilts her head, sighs, and whispers, "Thank you."

Flawed

My cock twitches, desperate for release. But then—

"Do you mind letting yourself out?"

I laugh. I think she's kidding.

"I'm still inside you and you're kicking me out?"

But her face changes. No humour. No softness. Just retreat.

She slides off me with a wince, pulling my hands away gently. Like I'm something she's finished with.

"Could you lock the door on your way out? I need to hop in the shower."

And then she's gone. Arms crossed. Walls rebuilt.

And I'm left kneeling on her bed, my heart pounding in my throat, cock ready to explode.

What the fuck just happened?

CHAPTER 10

ALLY

What the fuck just happened?

Seriously, I feel like my body just did something my brain didn't consent to. Not in the *someone took my control away* sort of way that sends me spiralling into panic. More like I was watching myself from the outside, completely detached. One moment, I was storming my way home, fuming over what Jax said, and the next… I'm naked in the shower, having just watched myself have sex with him.

The second the water hit me, I snapped back into myself—mind reeling, body aching, confused by the whirlwind of what just went down. I've had out-of-body experiences before, but nothing like this.

And the craziest part? I really enjoyed it.

I'm sore in ways I didn't think were possible, and I can already tell I'll be walking funny for days—but at that moment? *Fuck*. The way he looked at me, the way he touched me, the things he said—it was all so different. And my god, did I respond to him.

I can't quite wrap my head around why I reacted the way I did. Maybe it's just him—his touch, in all its forms. Or maybe I'm more open to things than I ever thought.

Like being called a whore? My subconscious mocks me while I mentally flip her off.

Whatever the reason, it felt life-affirming, and that's what's really messing with my head.

As I turn off the shower and wrap a towel around myself, I'm left wondering whether I should call an exorcist or Jeanie first. I step into my bedroom and I freeze.

Jax is sitting on the edge of my bed in unbuttoned jeans, his head in his hands.

Well this is awkward. I thought he'd be gone by now.

The surge of confidence I had during my dissociative moment vanishes entirely, leaving me acutely aware of just how inexperienced I am in… well, whatever this is.

I clear my throat, and he straightens up instantly, his gaze sweeping over me from head to toe. His hair's tousled in that freshly fucked way, and those lickable abs I remember so vividly are still very much on display, but his honey-coloured eyes—usually so playful—are serious now. That charming smirk I adore is nowhere in sight.

"You okay?" he asks.

I can only manage a slow nod, struggling to find actual words.

"Did I hurt you?" His voice is soft and laced with genuine concern. I want to say yes—you shattered my heart the last few weeks, but I decide to answer the question the way he meant it.

"I'm fine."

When I don't elaborate, a flicker of panic crosses his face.

"We didn't use protection."

Well, shit. That's exactly what you want to hear from a guy who slept his way through school.

"I've never forgotten before, I swear. I just… I got caught up in you," his voice drops, full of remorse. "I was tested not long ago for work. I'm clean."

I frown. "Why were you tested for work?" I can't help it—it seems odd, since he spends his days behind a computer.

"It's a government job. They do a full medical."

"I'm on the pill," I say, trying to keep my voice steady. "I haven't been tested in years, but I think it's safe to assume I'm clean."

He nods slowly, his face a strange mix of worry and uncertainty.

Silence stretches out between us, thick and heavy. Finally, I break it with a whisper, "What are you doing here?"

He looks at me, regret carved into every line of his

face.

"Ally, I'm really sorry. I never meant to hurt you." But I see the discomfort flicker in his eyes—we both know that's not entirely true.

"I'm sorry *that* I hurt you," he corrects.

When I stay silent, he continues, "Honestly, I've never been sorry for anything before in my life, but I regret the pain I caused you. I miss you, beautiful."

His eyes hold genuine sorrow, and I know he means it. It's written all over his face. But the real question lingers like a bitter taste in the back of my throat: Can I forgive him?

There's this enormous wall between us, built brick by brick with every lie he told. And yet… I miss him more than I want to admit. I miss that stupid, cocky smirk. The flutter in my chest when his name lights up my screen. Even the scent that clings to his clothes.

It sounds insane, considering everything that's happened, but those good memories are so vivid, they're hard to forget.

Still, the idea of letting him back in terrifies me. I can't stop replaying every deception, every omission.

How do you look someone in the eye and trust them again after they've shown you how easily they can lie?

I *want* to forgive him. I really do. But I feel trapped —caught—in this painful limbo between hope and caution. Maybe forgiveness isn't about forgetting… but how do you build something new on such a shaky foundation?

Is it even possible to miss someone enough to start over? To try knowing the real them instead of clinging to the fantasy?

I don't have the answer. Not yet. So I pivot.

"We should talk about the assault charges. Just give me a second to get dressed."

For a heartbeat, I see something shatter behind his eyes. Then he gathers himself, lets out a long breath.

"Honestly, I don't care about that. It's been weeks—if anything was going to happen, it would've by now."

When I stay quiet, he moves toward me, slowly— gently. He cradles my face, rests his forehead against mine.

I inhale sharply, drowning in the scent of him, the warmth of his skin, the tenderness in his touch.

And that's when it hits me: *I still feel safe with him.*

Just like that, the walls I built begin to crumble. I don't want to resist. I don't have the strength to keep pretending I don't still love him—even if the man I loved never really existed.

Because maybe I love him anyway. Flaws and all.

I've spent the last four years hiding behind a façade, burying parts of myself so deep no one could find them, until Jax peeled them back. And still, he accepts me.

Now it's my turn. Can I do the same for him?

"You need to promise to drop the act," I say, quietly. "Stop trying to be what you think I want."

He pulls back, eyes flicking between mine, searching. "What do you want?"

"I want to know you," I reply. "Not the polished version—the real you."

He hesitates, "You wouldn't like him. He's a proper cunt. Sam's so much better for you."

"You don't get to decide what's better for me," I snap. "Especially since I feel like I barely even know you. Seriously—do you even like peanut butter?"

It's a stupid question, but somehow it matters. I need

to know if anything I know about him is real.

He chuckles, just a little, and his thumb brushes my cheek. "Yeah. I do. The things you know about me haven't changed. Just… my perspective on the world has."

I search his face. "Can you promise to stop pretending?"

His thumb catches a tear I didn't realise had escaped, soft as a whisper. "But I make such a good fireman."

When I don't even crack a smile, he sighs.

"I'm not sure how to do that," he admits. "It's been so long since I've just been myself. But I promise I'll try."

I wrap my arms around his neck and press my lips to his. The kiss is soft, slow—so different from earlier. But it still sends shivers down my spine.

Because despite everything, I feel safe with him.

Later, Jeanie and I will rip this whole disaster apart, thread by thread—but for now?

I just want to stay right here, in his arms, and pretend —for a little while—that it's enough

Flawed

CHAPTER 11

JAX

Waking up in Ally's bed always feels like slipping into someone else's life—one where people wake up wrapped around someone they care about. It's the third morning I've woken up here, and instead of the usual post-fuck indifference, there's this gnawing sensation in my chest. I think it's affection. Or acid. Either way, I hate it.

Flawed

Last night, I let too much of the real me show, too fast. Told her she was being ridiculous for wanting to 'take it slow', like we hadn't already crossed every line she tries to draw. She blushed when she finally admitted she was sore from how hard I fucked her—and something about that stopped me cold. I don't want to hurt her. Not in ways that would make her pull emotionally away. That's new for me.

She stirs beside me, her leg brushing mine, and my hand moves to her waist without thinking. I pull her close, press my lips to her hair, and there it is again—that quiet, simmering sense that I want to protect her. It makes me feel sick. And yet I do it anyway.

"Morning, beautiful," I murmur, and she makes this soft, half-purring sound that goes straight to my cock. My body responds before my brain even catches up. She's still warm against me, tangled in the sheets, skin bare where the blanket's slipped—fuck, she's unreal.

I force myself to ease away from her warmth, jaw tight as I shift onto my side and push off the bed. Everything in me wants to stay pressed up against her, but I can't. Not unless I plan to take her again, and I shouldn't. Not yet.

My body protests as I sit up. The mattress dips, creaks. I curse under my breath, both at the physical ache and the fact that this girl—this fucking girl—has me so wound up I can barely breathe when she's near. She doesn't even have to touch me. Just existing next to me is enough to wreck me.

When I stand, I feel her eyes on my back, quiet, searching. Her brows knit together with that sweet concern she wears so easily, like she's trying to figure me out, piece by piece. As if I'm not made of sharp edges and locked doors.

Then she asks—innocent, soft, sweet—if I want help with my… situation.

My shoulders tense. I glance at her over my shoulder, and everything in me twists, caught between hunger and restraint.

She really has no idea what that offer does to me. That she'd even consider it—after everything I've said, everything she knows—I can't tell if she's mad, naive, or addicted. And god help her if it's the last one. Because I know exactly how to weaponise addiction.

But I don't. Not today.

"I'll sort myself out," I mutter, already turning away. "I've got to get to work anyway."

Weak. Transparent. There's no way she actually believes I'd rather jerk off alone than have her warm, willing mouth wrapped around me. She knows it. I know it. But we let the lie hang there.

She watches me, uncertain, that overthinking look already settling in—the one that says she'll replay this morning in her head a hundred different ways before lunch. I hate that I've put that look on her face. So I try to soften it.

I lean down, press a kiss to her shoulder, and murmur, "Dinner tonight? I've gotta hit the gym first, burn off some of this restless energy. But I'll meet you after?"

Her brow lifts, eyes playful now. "Is that why you go to the gym so much? To burn off energy?"

I huff a laugh, can't help it. "It's not like I got to come yesterday," I say, the words out before I can catch them.

Silence.

Her face twists—half shock, half something like hurt. Fuck. Wrong move.

She wants to see the real me? Well, here I am, folks. Raw and unfiltered. No mask. No charm. Just the part of me I usually keep hidden for good reason.

And now she's seen it.

"That was a joke," I quickly add, hoping to ease her discomfort, but she's not convinced.

"I go to the gym to keep my sanity intact," I add more honestly this time. I wish she understood the daily grind of someone like me, trying to navigate a world where people feel it's okay to chit chat and unload their personal dramas in a workplace.

That seems to pacify her, just enough for her to change the subject.

"Where do you want to go for dinner? I can meet you after work. Head back your way if that's easier. We could hit the pub near your place—less hassle for you," she says it so casually, but something about the suggestion puts me on edge.

I raise a brow. "Why would you want to go there?"

She shrugs. "You seem to enjoy it."

And that's when it hits me—she still believes there's a version of me worth doing normal things with. Pub dinners. Flirty bar staff. Jokes over pool. It's laughable, really.

"How much of the real me are you hoping to see?" I ask. A warning, not a test.

"All of him," she says, no hesitation.

So I peel back the mask.

"I like that pub because it's convenient for an easy fuck," I say flatly.

Her mouth opens, just barely. "But you said—"

"Ally, don't be daft. Of course I've fucked the bar staff."

She doesn't even flinch. Just blinks.

"So why take me there?" Her voice remains even, but something in her eyes shifts—like she's cataloguing, filing me away.

"Because she wouldn't stop texting me. I introduced you as my girlfriend to make her back off. And it made you feel special. Two birds, one stone."

I wait—for outrage, for tears, for anything.

But all she does is tilt her head, that same unreadable

calm in her face.

"Alright. Chinese then?"

She's not unbothered—no, that tight little smile gives her away—but she doesn't explode. Doesn't cry. Doesn't run. Just watches me with eyes that see too much.

"You're not mad?" I ask hesitantly.

Then she says something that will have me running circles around my own brain for the rest of the damn day.

"If I threatened to scratch your eyes out with a rusty fork and feed them to you every time you told me the truth, you'd never be honest with me. And that's not what I want."

What the fuck is this woman doing to me?

I just stare. For the first time in a long time, I have no idea what to say. This woman has me so captivated that I can't even form a coherent thought as I stand there, just gazing at her like a total fool. She's not supposed to be like this. She was meant to be fragile. Breakable. Mouldable.

But she's not. She's sharp. Steady. She's holding up a

mirror and daring me to keep looking, even when the reflection turns rotten.

I mumble some bullshit about needing to get to work and press a kiss to her lips. It's soft. Gentle. Not like me at all.

But the warmth it leaves behind? That fucking feeling sticks with me. Clings like guilt. Burns like pride.

And I know it's not love. I'm not wired for that. But it's something. Twisted. Primal. Possessive.

Something that snarls *mine*.

And the worst part?

I think I want her to keep digging, even if she unearths the monster I buried so deep, I almost forgot he has my face.

CHAPTER 12

ALLY

The second the door clicks shut behind him, I grab my phone to call Jeanie. Straight to voicemail.

Panic burns under my skin so I tap out an email, one word, all caps: SOS. No explanations. Just three letters loaded with everything I can't say out loud.

I pace the room while my mind continues to spin. My apartment feels too small to hold this much noise.

My phone buzzes.

Jax: You feeling ok, beautiful?

I suck in a breath, trying to centre myself. I can't let him see how shaken I am. If I'm really going to do this —get to know him, understand him—I need to hold it together.

Me: I'm fine. Why wouldn't I be?

Jax: Just checking in.

I slip into my silver glitter rain boots, hoping the sparkle might trick my brain into feeling lighter. The first few notes of *the bitch song* blast through my phone, and I can't help but laugh. Perfect timing.

"Hey, Ty."

"Hey. How'd last night go?" he asks.

Loaded question. How do I sum up a night like that?

"It went… okay, I think," I say carefully.

"You think?"

"We made up."

"You're seeing him again?" He sounds skeptical.

"Seeing him again or *seeing* him again?" I throw in a

little tease.

"Don't be cute."

"Yes to both."

There's a pause. Then—"Good. That's really good, Ally. I'm happy for you. Nate's gonna shit a brick, but it's all good."

Three goods in one sentence. That can't be *good*.

"What's wrong?" I ask, catching the tension in his voice.

"Nothing's wrong, exactly…"

"Ty. Spit it out."

He sighs. "Mum's throwing a party for Dad's birthday. I'm supposed to make sure you come."

"Absolutely not. Are you insane?"

"Come on, Ally. You're coming home for Christmas anyway."

"That's five months away. I'm not ready." My chest tightens.

"Don't be ridiculous," Ty says gently.

"I'm not ready to go back there," I repeat, more to myself than him.

He goes quiet. Usually we avoid this topic altogether,

he comes to me, not the other way around. But it was only a matter of time before the home conversation came up.

My relationship with our parents isn't strained, it's severed. They snapped that thread the day they told me to suck it up. When they dismissed my anxiety. When they cared more about their image than my survival.

And it's not just them—it's Newcastle. The whole place is haunted with a version of me I've spent years running from.

The silence stretches and when I blink and realise I'm crying.

"What if you brought Jax?" Ty says carefully. Like he believes Jax could magically fix everything. If only he knew the truth. I want to ask him, '*Which version of Jax*?' He's clearly thinking of the polished, well-rounded guy he's met, but I can't help but mentally chuckle at the thought of unleashing the raw, unfiltered Jax I encountered this morning on my hometown.

I laugh—a sharp, surprised bark. "What? You think if I bring him home, he'll finally realise I'm crazy enough to keep? Maybe he'll order my straightjacket in glitter."

"Ally. You're not crazy, and he doesn't think that either. Just… think about it."

We change the subject. Eventually, we're back to talking about last night, and I hang up feeling wrung out but oddly lighter.

I curl up on the couch with my laptop, letting fanfic soothe me—something ridiculous involving a lightning-struck shadow daddy and his accidental baby goat sidekick.

Just as I'm starting to relax, noon hits and my phone buzzes again.

Jax: Were you surprised you enjoy it rough?

My pulse spikes. I drop the phone like it burned me. *Jesus*.

Another buzz.

Jax: Don't go shy on me now. We're going to have so much fun with this ;)

Ally: Yes, I was surprised. No, I don't want to talk about it.

Jax: Haha. Can't wait to explore this with you.

My stomach flips, unsure if it's from nerves or anticipation.

By 7 PM, I'm in the lobby waiting for Jax. Jeanie and I just spent two hours on Zoom untangling my feelings, and to my shock, she's all for me giving this a shot. She even thinks I should go home. "Therapeutic," she said. Easy for her to say—she's never met my mother.

I sense Jax before I see him. Something about his energy wraps around me like static.

Then he's there, sweeping me up in his arms and dipping me into a Hollywood-style kiss. I giggle against his mouth, dizzy from the shift in gravity.

"Hey, beautiful."

"Hi yourself."

"We should probably go. Your concierge looks like he wants to throttle me."

Still dipped, I glance over and spot Paul glaring daggers. I laugh as Jax straightens me and takes my hand.

We head down the street. He walks past his car, and I trail behind, frowning, I can't shake the feeling that this might all be a show. He stops, turns, and brushes his knuckles down my cheek.

"Stop overthinking it," he says quietly. "I'm just as

confused as you are. Let's go with it."

I nod. Maybe that's the only choice we have.

"Dinner plans?"

"Burgers. I figured you could use some greasy comfort food after your long therapy session.

 I blink. "How'd you know I had therapy today?".

He smirks. "I dropped a psychological nuke on you. Of course you called your shrink. What'd she say?"

"Basically what you just did—get out of my head. Go with the flow. She wants to meet you."

He snorts. "Of course she does. A psychopath is a psychiatrist's wet dream."

I stop walking.

Something inside me short-circuits. The world tilts— just slightly, just enough. My hand slips from his, like my body knows something my brain hasn't caught up to yet. He turns to face me, brows pinched in confusion, reaching out again. I flinch.

His expression shifts. "Ally? You okay? You've gone pale."

He lifts a hand—just a knuckle near my cheek—and I flinch again. His eyes go cold.

"You're scared of me," he says, flat. Like he's already accepted it.

"I'm not," I lie. My voice trembles.

Am I?

Would he hurt me?

Would he *enjoy* it?

Is this the part where I find out he's been wearing a mask this whole time, and I'm the idiot who kissed it?

Can I run?

Would he let me?

What if he doesn't?

"Come here," he murmurs, pulling me into his arms before I can decide, before I can move.

And I let him. Because I don't know if clinging to the monster is safer than facing the dark alone.

I breathe him in. Sandalwood and safety. Slowly, my arms wrap around him. No—deep down—I know I'm not afraid *of* him. I'm afraid of what he is to me.

Dinner's easy. Too easy. I laugh too much. Relax too quickly. But in the back of my mind, I'm dissecting everything, measuring every word for sincerity.

It's almost two hours in when he leans back and

grins.

"So, are we just pretending your dad's birthday isn't coming up, or…?"

"Are you actually psychic?" I laugh, but his reaction —the stiff smile, the hair ruffle—makes my stomach tighten.

"How do you even know about that?"

"Tyler called me."

"You talk to my brother?"

"Not like we're pen pals but he called me today. He wants you to go and thinks you will if I go with you."

"How the hell does he even have your number?" I ask, eyebrows raised in disbelief.

Jax shrugs like it's nothing. "I message him sometimes."

"You what?"

"Just to check in on you," he says it so casually, like we're discussing the weather. "He knows you better than I do. I'm afraid I'll miss something subtle… something important about your mental state."

Anger prickles under my skin. "Why do you even care?"

His tone softens. "Because it's about you. Of course I care."

I don't respond.

"If you want to go, I'll come with you. No pressure."

He looks almost nervous. It's oddly sweet.

"I don't know if I'm ready." I admit, staring down at my lap. Embarrassment crawls up my neck, hot and prickling. I can't bring myself to meet his eyes.

He reaches across the table, lacing his fingers with mine like it's the most natural thing in the world.

"I'll keep you safe. No way I'm letting you face that alone."

God help me—I believe him.

"Okay. I'm in."

"Two weekends away?"

"Yeah. Saturday to Sunday. We will have to stay at my parents', separate rooms though. My mother will berate me for being a whore if I stay in a hotel with you… and Ty's place is too small."

He smirks. "But you like being called a whore."

"Oh my god, Jax."

"Come on. Admit it. You loved it."

"I did not."

"Your cunt flooded and you came almost instantly. Don't lie. Firemen are catnip for good girls with filthy fantasies."

I bury my face in my hands, half mortified, half thrilled.

◆ ◆ ◆

The walk back to my apartment feels… off. Jax pulls me to the inside of the sidewalk, like he's done before, but this time, I don't brush it off as a sweet habit. The first time, I thought it was chivalry. Now? I'm not so sure.

He catches the shift in my expression and speaks before I can ask.

"I'll always keep you safe, Ally. You're mine to protect."

It's possessive. Intense. And fuck me, it works.

But the anxiety's creeping in again.

What if I'm wrong about him? What if he's dangerous?

We reach the building. My voice is barely a whisper, "I had a nice time."

When he leans in, I flinch again.

His hands curl into fists. His jaw tightens. *Fuck, he's angry.*

"Are you okay?"

The edge in his voice cuts like glass.

"Yeah. Just… not feeling great."

His eyes flash. "Whatever. I had a shit time anyway." He turns and stalks off.

I hurry into my building and apartment and don't breathe until the door locks behind me.

Then I grab my laptop and email Jeanie. It's short and to the point.

Still wired, I open a search tab and type one word: Psychopath.

Definition: Personality disorder characterised by a set of dysfunctional interpersonal, emotional, lifestyle, and antisocial tendencies…

Traits:

- Lack of guilt or empathy
- Pretends to feel emotions
- Inability to form attachments
- Manipulative, narcissistic

Flawed

- Superficial charm

JESUS. FUCKING. CHRIST.

CHAPTER 13

JAX

She's fucking scared of me.

I put in so much effort to make her feel secure—every calculated move, every soft touch, every steady breath—and then I go and make one stupid, unfiltered, psychopath comment. And now she's scared of me.

I'm gripping the steering wheel so tight I think it

might crack under the pressure. Anger floods through me—hot, wild, uncontrollable. I want to hit something, break something, feel something other than this twisted cocktail of regret and rage.

By the time I get home, I can't decide if I want to destroy the punching bag in the garage or snoop through her emails like the pathetic, lovesick idiot I've apparently turned into.

I end up racing up the stairs two at a time like a man possessed, straight into my home office. I don't even sit down before logging in. I need to know what's going on inside her head.

I log into her email, fingers suddenly heavy on the keys.

Straight to the sent folder.

And there it is.

The subject line hits me like a fucking freight train.

Loud. Brutal. Unavoidable.

HE'S A FUCKING PSYCHO.

The body of the email hits me just as hard.

Not a joke. Not a heat-of-the-moment insult. A literal assessment.

Is that all I am to her now?

My hands curl into fists at my sides. I'm losing my grip on the anger. I need to act. I need to see her.

I don't even hesitate. It's too easy to tap into her webcam. One of the perks of being me—most people don't know how vulnerable they really are.

She's sitting there, eyes scanning something on her screen. Then she starts typing. Pauses. Reads. Her expressions shift—concentration, doubt, maybe fear.

What is she reading?

Digging into her search history is harder, but I'm not exactly a stranger to digital trespassing.

The definition of a psychopath.

Common traits.

Can they experience feelings?

Are they dangerous?

Can they become violent?

What are they capable of?

Psychopaths sexual behaviour traits.

Fuck!

She isn't scared of *me*. She's scared of what I *could* become. She's scared of what I might already be.

Flawed

Her trauma runs deep. Deeper than I ever let myself acknowledge. Someone she trusted before me broke her in ways she doesn't talk about, not fully. Hurt her physically. Left her afraid of people who are supposed to love her.

And now? She's looking at me through that same lens.

Tonight, I saw it, that flicker of fear in her eyes when I touched her. She recoiled, just for a second. But it felt like a gut punch. Like she was bracing for a blow. For me to disappear again. For me to explode.

She thinks I'm a ticking time-bomb. A walking stereotype. Some cold, calculated threat who will shatter her the second she lets her guard down.

I can't let that happen. I *won't*.

Because I don't just want her body anymore. I want her heart, her fear, her rage, her ruin—everything.

Every move I make from now on has to be intentional. Measured. Predictable. Gentle. But how the fuck do I balance that with being myself? With letting her see who I really am—without triggering every fear she's spent years trying to bury?

How do you erase someone else's trauma?

How do you convince someone you're not the monster they're scared of, especially when that fear is based on real pain? Will this be a constant battle? Will she ever trust me again? When your darkness fits the description too well?

I'm terrified. Terrified that I won't win this fight. That I'll lose her, even if my heart is in the right place.

Because like a goddamn idiot, in a moment of reckless passion, I fucked her like she was mine to break.

And now? Is it really a surprise that she fears me?

My hand moves before I even register it, grabbing my phone.

Jax: I would never hurt you. Not again.

I glance back at the screen. Her phone lights up. She picks it up slowly, brows furrowing. And then, her lips curve.

Just a little.

Ally: I believe you..

CHAPTER 14

ALLY

I AM NOT CRAZY.

This motherfucker isn't psychic—he's in my fucking computer. For months it seems.

Jeanie, I want to chat more with Jax but don't know how to approach it.

Jax: *Sweet dreams, Ally x*

Jeanie, should I judge him for his past? Lord knows

I've made mistakes in mine.

*   **Jax***: What's the stupidest thing you ever did?*

*   Jeanie, he treats sex like a sport.*

*   **Jax***: I now understand the value of physical intimacy.*

*   Jeanie, I've outlined my goals for my five-year plan.*

*   **Jax***: Where do you see yourself in five years?*

*   Jeanie, my head says run but my heart says stay.*

*   **Jax***: What's more influential? Your brain or your heart?*

*   Jeanie, I need an emergency zoom.*

*   **Jax***: I dropped a psychological nuke on you. Of course you called your shrink.*

He knew everything. Didn't flinch when Ty called me Hannah. Didn't blink when I clung to him like a lifeline during our post-attack breakfast adventure.

I thought he was being patient. Understanding. Gentle.

Nope.

He just already knew. All of it.

I should be pissed. Fuming. Livid. But instead… I'm smiling like a lovestruck idiot. Because this deranged level of digital invasion? Kind of weirdly romantic.

Flawed

Sure, we're going to have a very serious conversation about boundaries and consent, but for now? I'm flattered. Freaked out. But flattered.

He's already fucked me—game over—and he still cares this much? Enough to hack my digital existence?

I honestly don't know whether to scream or swoon.

But two can play this game.

Hey Jeanie,

I feel like I should elaborate on my last email now that I've had a moment to process. Right now, I'm stuck in some chaotic whirlpool of feelings. I understood what he meant when he said he doesn't feel things the usual way, but it didn't hit me until he used the actual terminology. It makes sense now.

Do you think that's why the sex was so... meh? I mean, I tried to keep an open mind, but a fake orgasm is still a fake orgasm. I even did the little breathy gasp at the end and everything.

Maybe I hyped it up too much in my head after all the books I've read? But it was just... disappointing. No hard feelings—'its not his fault he's working with a travel-sized penis and the stamina of a squirrel on Red

Bull. I'm just thinking maybe it's time to move on. Find someone who doesn't finish during the opening credits and knows where a clitoris lives.

I hit send and slump back into the couch, grinning like a smug little gremlin. Seconds later, my phone lights up.

Jax: Wipe that stupid smile off your face. I know you're full of shit.

What. The. Fuck.

He can see me?

I whip my head around, scanning the room for cameras, shadows, cloaked stalkers in the closet.

Then—buzz.

Jax: Stop freaking out. IT extraordinaire, remember? Only I can see you.

My eyes snap to the webcam. That tiny, unassuming little circle at the top of my laptop suddenly feels like a thousand-watt spotlight.

And yet... I smirk.

God help me, I *smirk*.

What is wrong with me?

Instead of throwing the laptop across the room like a

normal person with boundaries, I tip my head, fluff my hair like I'm in a Pantene commercial, and say, "Enjoy the show, creeper."

This is it. This is how Stockholm Syndrome starts. Not with chains or dungeons, but with snarky texts and dangerously sexy surveillance.

And worse? I like it.

I feel my nipples tighten, a rush of heat pooling between my thighs like my body missed the memo about boundaries.

Grinning, I lift the hem of my shirt—slow, deliberate, teasing. Fingers slip just under the cup of my bra, giving him the briefest flash of pink before I tug everything back into place like nothing happened.

Then I flip the bird straight at the camera.

"Enjoy the mental image, perv," I mutter, slamming the laptop shut with a satisfying snap.

If he wants to play, I'll play.

But I *always* play to win.

Jax: Cheeky little tease. Get some sleep, beautiful. I'll talk to you tomorrow x.

Ally: Sweet dreams x.

Flawed

After a long, hot shower, I crawl into bed, brain still doing cartwheels from the emotional gymnastics that is Jax Beckett. In the span of one evening, he managed to be charming dinner date, sulky teenager, and casually possessive cyber-stalker—like a one-man theatre production with zero warning and no intermission.

And honestly? I'm not even mad about it.
God help me, I might actually be into it.

◆ ◆ ◆

The next day's a blur of texting and overanalysing.

Jax kicks things off with a "good morning, beautiful," like we didn't end the night with mild emotional whiplash and light surveillance kink.

Then Jeanie gets involved. Naturally.

I get grilled over zoom—about my sexually underwhelment, and then my emotionally volatile hacker boyfriend. We spiral into a half-hour analysis of Jax's mental state. She's not shocked by anything I say, which I'm starting to realise is either her being a professional… or just deeply unshockable.

I walk her through my evening with the many personalities of Jax—the charmer, the moody teenager, and casually possessive stalker, all rolled into one six-foot something enigma. Her official diagnosis? A toddler with Wi-Fi and zero parental controls. That's Jax—emotionally constipated and just now buffering his way through feelings in real time. When he doesn't get his way or some unfamiliar emotion glitches the system, he short-circuits like a kid in the middle of the terrible twos: throws a tantrum, slams a metaphorical door, a full emotional shutdown like someone yanked his batteries out and walked off. She's not thrilled about the webcam incident. But she understands why I didn't scream and throw my laptop into the sea. We compromise: no more emails. Texts only.

Mid-sneaker shopping online, my phone pings.

Jax: I like the yellow ones, beautiful.

I glance at my laptop, still open on the counter, and smirk.

Ally: Me too. I'm buying them when I get back.

Jax: Where you off to, beautiful?

Ally: Just grabbing lunch.

Jax: Have fun x.

The whole way to the café, I can't stop thinking about it. How it doesn't bother me. How it kinda… thrills me. That twisted, possessive energy of his? It's messed up. But it makes me feel seen. Wanted. In a way I didn't realise I was starving for.

I grab coffee and sandwiches—on Jax's dime, of course he topped up my account (he's about as subtle as a brick). Then I head to the park to find Will.

◆ ◆ ◆

Back home, I'm feeling good. Comfortable. A little too smug.

I change into something cute, fix my hair, touch up my makeup, and cozy up on the couch to look for my next project when my phone buzzes.

Jax: You were gone a while.

Ally: Had lunch with Will.

Jax: Who the fuck is Will?

Flawed

I glance at the webcam and laugh out loud.

Ally: Nice guy from the park. You bought him food
last week. I brought him lunch.

Jax: I'll be over after work!

Oh, it's on.

CHAPTER 15

JAX

Just four fucking words. Four words that make my blood run cold and my vision blur with red. *Had lunch with Will.*

I stare at the screen, unblinking, heart pounding like a war drum. The rational part of my brain, the one trained to read signals and respond with precision, has already been drowned in a tidal wave of rage. I can't think, I can only spiral.

Why didn't she tell me?

Was he flirting with her?

Is he making her laugh like *I* do?

No. No. No.

I dig my fingers into the edge of my desk until my knuckles crack. I picture him—this Will—smiling at her, maybe leaning in a little too close, maybe brushing her wrist like it's nothing. Like she's available.

She's not.

She's *mine*.

I should call her. I should calmly ask about her day like a normal boyfriend. But I'm not a normal boyfriend. I'm the monster under the bed, the one you forget to fear until it's too late. So I sit there instead, seething, silent, boiling from the inside out.

I simmered in my frustration, replaying every recent conversation in my mind, desperately searching for signs that I was losing her, that she was already on her way out.

If I were working from home, I'd already be at her door. Or in her bed. Or going through her phone while she showers.

But I'm stuck in this fucking office, watching her through the security feed as she navigates a new job bid. She's smiling—smiling—as she clicks through the won contract for some god awful book about a soccer-playing heroin addict.

Seriously, who writes this shit?

At least I know she's home now.

Unless Will followed her back.

Unless she invited him in.

Unless her bed smells like him.

Is it irrational to be this mad over a man who calls a park bench his mattress? Fuck yes. But is the rational part of my brain currently clocked in? Nope. He has packed a bag, flipped me the bird, and left me alone with my *feelings* and a bottle of dumb-cunt juice.

I close the feed and shut my laptop before I break it in half.

Five o'clock can't come soon enough.

♦ ♦ ♦

Flawed

The second the clock ticks over, I'm out of my chair and halfway to her place. I blow past her concierge without a word, jaw tight, fists clenched. If he tried to stop me, I'd lay him out on the marble floor without blinking.

She opens the door a second after I knock, probably startled by the force of it.

Good.

I don't wait.

I step inside, slam the door shut with my boot, and grab her.

My hands are in her hair, on her throat, dragging her mouth to mine. She tastes like mint and sunshine, and something I can't name but crave like oxygen. I push her against the wall, pinning her arms above her head with one hand while the other grips her jaw, forcing her to look at me.

"Did you have *fun* with Will?" I ask, a low snarl against her lips.

Her eyes go wide. "It was just—"

I silence her with my mouth, devouring the rest of her answer because it doesn't matter. I don't care. I just need her moaning into me, writhing under me, forgetting anyone else exists.

She melts, like she always does. Her surrender is instant and intoxicating.

Clothes come off fast—ripped, tugged, tossed without care. I drag her into the bedroom and throw her on the bed like a doll. She gasps, but I see the heat flash in her eyes. She likes it. She wants more.

Good. Because I'm not giving her softness tonight.

Her tights tear like paper in my hands. I strip her down to her black lace underwear, the sight of it making my cock throb in my jeans. I peel them off slowly, deliberately, watching her bite her lip as I take in every inch of bare skin.

"You've been teasing me all day," I growl, crawling over her. "And now you're going to take every fucking inch I give you."

I grip her thighs, spread them wide, and sink two fingers into her heat. She's soaked already—of course she is. Her body knows who owns it.

I bring my fingers to my mouth, tasting her. My eyes never leave hers.

"You taste like sin," I whisper. "I'm going to eat you alive later. Right now? I need to ruin you."

I strip down fast, freeing my cock with a desperate urgency. Her eyes flick down, pupils dilating, and she shifts her hips, inviting me in.

"Please," she breathes.

That's all it takes.

I slam into her with no warning, one hand gripping her throat while the other pins her hip to the mattress. She cries out—high and breathless—but she doesn't tell me to stop. She never does. Her body arches into mine, her legs wrap tight around my waist as I pound into her like I'm trying to break us both.

"Harder," she begs.

I give it to her—hips snapping, cock dragging against her walls with brutal precision. I reach between us, circle her clit in tight, punishing strokes. Her back bows. Her nails rake down my back, and I hiss through my teeth as she clenches around me, trembling on the edge.

"Come for me, Ally." My voice is harsh. Commanding. I need her to fall apart first. I need her to know I can do this to her—over and over and over again.

She shatters, screaming my name, and I keep going.

I flip her over, raise her ass, and slide back in with a grunt. She's still twitching, whimpering, her legs weak beneath her. Bending over her, I wrap my arm around her waist, bring my thumb to her lips.

"Suck."

She obeys instantly, tongue soft and obedient.

I trail the hand thumb down her back, circling her tight virgin hole causing her to tense.

"Jax?" she squeaks, her voice laced with a mix of concern and vulnerability.

"Relax," I whisper, kissing her spine. "Trust me."

I press the tip of my thumb inside and she gasps—a helpless, overwhelmed sound—and when she doesn't push me away, I go deeper. Her pussy clenches around me, tighter than ever.

I groan. I lose it.

With my cock inside her cunt and my thumb buried in her ass, I pull her upright against my chest. Her head falls back, mouth open, and I bite her neck hard enough to leave a mark she won't be able to hide.

"Jax," she cries.

And then she breaks again.

I fuck her through it, relentless, watching her collapse into submission with every thrust.

When I feel myself getting close, I pull out with a growl and come all over her ass—thick, hot, *claiming*. My mark. My warning. My fucking flag in the dirt.

Breathing heavily, I collapse beside her, drawing her close so her head rests comfortably on my chest. I run my fingers through her hair, tucking it behind her ear as I savour the afterglow.

"That was incredible," she whispers, still catching her breath. I can't help but smile at her response.

"I'd appreciate you telling Jeanie about it," I tease, and she laughs, snuggling deeper into me.

She starts to move—probably to clean up—but I pull her back down into me, arms wrapped around her like a vice.

"I need a shower," she whispers.

I kiss her shoulder, still panting. "No you don't. I'm going to rub it into your skin so you can't wash it off."

She hums, sleepy and satisfied, already melting into

my chest.

My hand slides over the curve of her ass, spreading the mess across her skin with slow, possessive strokes.

"You're mine, Ally," I whisper against her hair. "Mine. And I'll destroy anyone who forgets that."

CHAPTER 16

ALLY

So, I think Jax lives here now.

He showed up on Tuesday night and just… never left. That was six days ago. He did duck out briefly on Thursday for work, but he came right back without any warning—just a small duffle bag and an annoyed look like he'd been gone too long already. His toothbrush has taken up permanent residence in my bathroom. He moves around my kitchen like it's his own. A new coffee mug showed up by day three. There's a razor in the shower now. It's almost comical, like watching a slow, steady invasion—adorable and terrifying all at once.

He's never said the words *I'm moving in,* but he doesn't need to. His presence is louder than any declaration, and if I'm being honest, I don't hate it. I might even love it. Him.

It's strange how little has changed between us since I learned the truth. You'd think discovering your boyfriend casually identifies as a psychopath would send you running for the hills, or at least flinching every time he gets too quiet. But I don't. Not even close.

He's still Jax. Still the same man who overuses fireman puns and puts peanut butter on literally everything. He still makes me laugh when I'm mid-breakdown and still somehow always knows when I need water, caffeine, or to be railed against the fridge—sometimes all three.

But there is a difference. A shift. Like someone took a black charcoal pencil and sketched in shadows around the edges of him that I hadn't noticed before. His perceptiveness? Not empathy—it's calculation. His patience? Not kindness—control. And yet... he's still him. Or at least, the version of him I've grown impossibly attached to. It's unsettling, this duality—how someone can be both a safe place and a threat, a shelter and a storm.

And apparently, I like storms.

The only time he actually scares me is when work goes sideways. Captain Perfectionist does *not* handle unsolvable code well. He gets irrational—rude in that cold, clinical way—and shuts down so hard he won't even talk to me.

Not because he's angry at me, but because he doesn't trust what might come out of his mouth.

Instead, he texts me from across the room.

"Typing it gives me a chance to process and filter what I say," he explained.

Which is honestly both horrifying and weirdly considerate. Romance is dead. Long live the emotionally constipated psychopath with a Wi-Fi plan and the emotional range of a teaspoon.

Flawed

We've fallen into a strange rhythm. Every morning, he makes coffee and hands me a mug without asking how I take it. Every night, we orbit toward the kitchen around the same time, somehow always ready to cook, even if we don't speak. He still texts me questions at noon every day, even when I'm sitting two feet away. I've also noticed his laptop always has the webcam feed open, minimised but never closed.

He watches me. I should be disturbed by that, but I'm not. Maybe because I know I'd do the same if it were him.

The other day he came with me to lunch with Will, and it was clear from the second we sat down that Jax's presence wasn't about social niceties. He barely spoke— just glared and growled at Will under his breath, and then spent the rest of the time buried in his phone. It's ridiculous for him to feel this way about a manwho's possessions fit into garbage bag but as soon as we got home, he pinned me to the wall and fucked me like he was erasing any trace of someone else touching me. His hand wrapped around my throat, then he shoved me to my knees and came all over my chest, rubbing it into my skin like he was painting his name on me. He wouldn't let me shower for hours after. He just held me, arms tight around my waist, his voice low in my ear, *Mine.*

And here's the part I'm struggling to understand.

I liked it.

I shouldn't. Not after everything I went through. Not after being taken without choice, without control. That kind of ownership should send me spiralling, should rip open old wounds that still haven't fully healed. But it didn't. With Jax, it's different. The roughness, the dominance—it doesn't feel like a violation. It feels like freedom.

Which makes no sense, right?

I keep telling myself it's because it's him. I trust Jax in ways that scare me. I trust him enough to hand him the reins and let myself feel. I know he'd never cross a line I didn't secretly want him to. I know he watches me closer than I even watch myself, always checking for signs, always reading the smallest flinch. He pushes me, yes, but only as far as I let him. And maybe that's what makes the difference.

It's not that I like being dominated.

It's that I like *him* dominating me.

That I trust him to take me there and bring me back safely.

I used to imagine my sex life—if I ever dared to have one—would be soft. Gentle. Vanilla enough to lull my nervous system into submission. But Jax doesn't do soft. He does feral. He doesn't ask with words—he asks with eyes, with touch, with tension so thick I can barely breathe. He commands, and I obey, and somewhere in that obedience, I feel… strong. Like I'm not broken anymore. Like I'm more me than I've ever been.

The most unexpected part? Since he started staying over, I haven't had a single nightmare.

Not one.

And sure, maybe it's the physical exhaustion from constantly fucking like we're trying to break the laws of biology. His rebound time is absurd. Pornographic. He's always ready for more, and I keep letting him. Wanting him. Needing him.

He brings up anal at least once a day. I always laugh it off, and he pouts like a petulant child denied dessert. But it's about letting someone see every part of you, even the ones you've buried under shame or discomfort. It feels like the final frontier. More intimate than anything we've done, even the things I never imagined myself doing at all.

He says it's a trust thing. He's wrong.

It's a me thing. A 'do I love myself enough to let someone love all of me?' thing.

It makes me self-conscious, like I'm standing at the edge of a line I've drawn in thick, anxious ink. Crossing it feels too taboo, too raw.

I'm not there yet. But I think I'm getting closer.

And that? That's scarier than anything he's ever done to me in bed.

It's a Monday night, and I'm tidying up after dinner when my phone starts ringing. The caller ID makes me hesitate. I just stand there, staring at the screen, frozen, until Jax's voice cuts through my daze.

"What's wrong?"

I keep my eyes on the glowing screen and answer flatly, "Nothing, I'm fine."

I hit the answer button and bring the phone to my ear just as my mother's voice slices through the air.

"Hello, *Hannah*."

Her tone is soaked in sarcasm—just hearing the name feels like a slap.

"Hi," I whisper, instantly feeling twelve years old again. It's been months of silence, and yet she slips right back into her role like no time has passed.

"Well, this is a surprise. Decided to stop pretending and come home, have you?"

"I'm only coming for the night."

"Always with the flair for drama."

I bite down on the inside of my cheek.

"Tyler said you're bringing someone with you?"

"My boyfriend."

She lets out a low, cynical chuckle.

"How convenient," she says, slowly. "Tyler seems to think he's quite something." She laughs, soft and clipped, like she finds the idea amusing but a little sad.

"He is, actually,"

"Oh, I'm sure he is, sweetheart. Just—try not to scare him off."

I go still, eyes locked on the bench.

"You do have a habit of getting… complicated."

Flawed

Her words feel like a punch to the chest.

"Who are you talking to?" Jax's voice is sharp, slicing through my spiralling thoughts. His gaze locks onto mine—calm, but burning. He strides over, plucks the phone from my hand, glances at the screen, and hangs up. No hesitation. Then he cups my face gently and kisses me before pulling me into his arms.

"I don't know what she said, but I don't want you talking to anyone who makes you look this sad."

"Looks like it's going to be a long weekend," I murmur.

The phone rings again. Jax silences it without a word, then returns to wrap himself around me like a shield. The rest of the night passes in a blur. He runs me a hot shower, then fucks me into distraction against the tiled wall.

Afterwards, I crawl into bed and fall asleep in the arms of a man I can't help but think might be far too good for me. Even with his flaws.

The night is strange. The moon is too bright in a starless sky, casting an eerie silver sheen across everything. I stand barefoot at the entrance of a hedge maze, the grass cold and wet under my feet. My gold sneakers are gone—how, I don't know.

A gust of wind cuts behind me, and I hear my name whispered in the dark, soft and sinister. I don't turn around.

I take a step into the maze. The hedges tower over me, creaking as though they're alive and watching. The air is heavy with the scent of decay. I wrap my arms around myself, fighting the panic already beginning to curl through my chest.

The path ahead twists unnaturally, and then I hear it —slow, heavy footsteps following me. I can't see anyone. I walk faster. The footsteps keep pace. I break into a run, gravel biting at the soles of my feet. The hedges shift behind me, paths vanishing. I trip on a root and fall hard, my knee splitting open. Warm blood trickles down my leg.

The hedge brushes against my skin—it licks at my wound. I try to scream, but no sound comes out. I stumble into a clearing bathed in moonlight, where my cracked pearl headband lies on the ground. As I reach for it, something grabs my ankle.

I whirl around. Nothing there. Just shadows.

Clutching the headband, I run. The maze tightens. Ahead, something moves, tall and contorted, all the wrong angles. It looks like me. And it's smiling.

A mirror appears in the hedge. My reflection stares back, calm, collected... wearing my gold glitter sneakers. It waves.

Then I hear my own voice whisper behind me, "You never left."

I wake with a scream, lungs on fire, heart hammering against my ribs. Hands grip my shoulders. I flinch and fight their hold.

"Ally, it's okay. You're okay. I'm here," Jax's voice is low and firm, anchoring me.

I've woken him. My skin's slick with sweat, hair sticking to my face. He eases his grip, brushing my hair back, trying to soothe me. His eyes are wide with concern—he isn't annoyed I woke him. He's scared. That almost feels worse.

Overwhelmed, I scramble from the bed, shedding

clothes as I bolt. I lock myself in the bathroom, turn on the shower, and step under the freezing water before it's even warm. I scrub my skin like it'll wipe the dream from my mind, the door handle rattling behind me.

I close my eyes and stand there, letting the water wash over me.

And then his hands are on my hips. He presses his body to my back, rests his chin on my shoulder. He doesn't speak for a while.

"I don't like it when you run from me," he says eventually, quiet and calm.

I don't answer.

"What happened in there?"

"I'm sorry I woke you."

"Least of my worries right now."

"I'm sorry I scared you."

He snorts. "Sweetheart, I *am* the thing that goes bump in the night. Takes a lot more than that to scare me."

That earns a smile from me. I turn to face him, resting my hands on his chest.

"You're not so scary," I tease.

He grins. "Must be losing my touch. I'll have to try harder." He kisses my nose gently.

"Must be nice not being scared of anything," I whisper, heat creeping up my neck. He tilts my chin up with his knuckle.

"There is something," he says, lowly. "I'm scared of losing you. Terrified, actually. When you run like that, I never know if it means your wall's going back up… and maybe next time, you won't come back to me."

It's amazing how this beautifully flawed man can seem so perfect when I'm at my most broken. I know, on some level, this is him being Sam—the master manipulator—but right now? I need him. And he knows that. He always knows.

"I love you, Ally. As best as I know how to."

We spend the rest of the early morning tangled in each other. He falls asleep with his arm around me, steady and warm. I stay awake, curled into him, feeling just a little less scared about the weekend ahead.

CHAPTER 17

JAX

It's Friday morning, and for the first time in over a week, I'm forced to untangle myself from Ally's bed and play the part of a functional adult.

Two back-to-back design meetings on a project that apparently can't survive without me.

I stay wrapped around her longer than I should,

ignoring the gym and the ticking clock. I don't have the right clothes here—just jeans and tees—but if the Suits at work have a problem with it, they can go cry about it in HR. I'm good at what I do, and they know it. I don't need a blazer to prove it.

The morning flies, mostly because I've buried myself in tasks, trying not to think about the soft weight of her in my arms last night or the way she flinched awake like she was being dragged back from the dead. Again.

I had to shut down the live webcam feed from her apartment—couldn't exactly explain *that* to my team. But whenever someone's distracted, I sneak a glance. Just enough to check in.

She's curled up on the couch, laptop in her lap, eyebrows scrunched as she reads about some rodeo clown with a fucked knee.

She smiles and starts to laugh at the script.

What goes on in that head of hers?

It's unnerving how quickly she has infected my life. I even tolerate my coworkers now, which is a clear sign of mental decline. Normally I'd be daydreaming about holding their heads under water just long enough to panic. Today? Just minor violence. Broken noses. Maybe a dislocated jaw if someone really earns it.

Truth is, I'm stuck in a kind of limbo—desperate for the weekend to arrive, but dreading what it means for her.

Three nights in a row of screaming herself awake, clawing at the sheets like she's still trapped wherever her dreams take her.

She won't say it, but going home is eating her alive.

She's been quieter. Not cold, just… distant. Like she's trying to keep herself from unraveling in front of me.

I've called Sam in more times than I care to admit. Not because I can't handle her, but because I want to do right by her. She doesn't even argue anymore. Deep down, she knows I'm right. She needs it.

And I don't give a fuck if she resents me for it. I'll coddle her delusions if it's necessary.

Watching her slowly fall apart is fucking exhausting. She's biting her nails until they bleed, drinking when she thinks I'm not paying attention, eyes hollowed out by exhaustion and fear. She's drowning herself in deadlines and caffeine and this compulsive need to pretend she's okay.

What kills me is how afraid she is to let me see her break. Last night, she finally cracked and admitted it—told me she didn't want to weigh me down with her 'emotional baggage' because I 'don't do emotions.'

She's not wrong, but that doesn't mean I don't care. It's twisted, the way I feel it—like an itch in my veins—but I do.

For her.

I regret letting her know I was checking her emails. Not because I care about privacy, but because it's made her hold back with her therapist. They still text, but it's surface-level now. Performative.

She has a Zoom session scheduled today, but she hasn't said a word. Maybe she's hoping to be okay by the time it rolls around. Wishful thinking.

Her brother has been checking in every day. That used to annoy me—someone hovering around what's mine—but now, I'm just grateful. She deflects, lies through her teeth, and he still calls. He even reached out to me yesterday.

I was careful—honest enough to raise concern, vague enough not to betray her. He said she's her own worst enemy. That once the darkness sets in, she disappears inside it until she's ready to claw her way out.

I hate that I can't drag her out of it myself.

She was fucking adorable yesterday, all nervous and blushing, trying to ask if I could be 'Sam' for just the weekend.

"I know it's kind of hypocritical," she mumbled, eyes flicking away. "And I don't want you to be someone you're not, but… maybe don't let my parents know you're one of the monsters who lives under the bed? Also, they really don't need to know that your favourite words are fuck and cunt."

I nearly choked on my coffee. The fact that she thinks I can pass as anything *but* the monster under the bed is fucking hilarious. Assuming I'd tone it down just because her mother might clutch her pearls made my day.

I told her I'd play the part—Mr. Wholesome and Respectable—for forty-eight hours.

As long as I got to bend her over something nostalgic

in her childhood bedroom.

She didn't laugh. Too wired to find me funny.

I overheard her talking to her dad last night. He doesn't seem like the asshole her mother clearly is.

When she whispered to him to ensure there was peanut butter at home, thinking I wasn't listening, I nearly fucking melted.

She turned scarlet when she caught me smiling at her. That shyness of hers is infuriatingly cute.

The same girl who can scream my name while I wreck her against the headboard gets flustered admitting she's on her period.

The other day, when I got too close, she panicked, grabbed a spatula like she was about to fend off a home invasion. I should've backed off, but her face was too good. Full red-cheeked meltdown. I figured out what was going on quite quickly, but decided to drag it out, play dumb, and watch her squirm. Entertainment value? Off the charts.

By the time she finally choked the words out, I was doubled over laughing with actual tears. She then proceeded to actually assault me with the damn spatula.

Repeatedly.

Naturally, I fireman-carried her to the shower and dumped her in, fully clothed.

Told her I was gonna fuck her unplugged.

She did not appreciate the pun—until I started peeling off her wet clothes and made her forget her own name.

Pro tip: never call your menstruating girlfriend 'Code Red.' Turns out, it's not endearing. Or sexy. Or—according to her—"Remotely fucking funny, Jax, do you want to die today?"

"Jackson, can this be done in three weeks?"

Lila's voice cuts through my thoughts like nails on glass. She's smirking, all false sweetness and passive threat.

I have no idea what she's referring to. Probably some bullshit rollout that would take a miracle.

But I won't flinch.

"Absolutely."

My team groans. Programmers—always so realistic. Pity.

Lila blinks, caught off guard. She was hoping I'd

argue. Now she's looking at me like I just grew wings.

She's giving me that look again. The one she thinks is seductive. It's not. It makes my skin crawl.

I shouldn't have fucked her at that Christmas party. I thought it would give me leverage—some insurance policy if she ever tried to pull rank, especially considering how seriously the company enforces its 'no fraternising' policy.

I was wrong and now, she thinks we're playing a game. One I'm no longer interested in.

Just as the meeting's winding down, there's a knock at the boardroom door.

Two men step inside. Everyone's attention turns.

Then their eyes find me.

Well, fuck.

CHAPTER 18

ALLY

The clock on my phone mocks me with every passing second, dragging time out like it knows how close I am to breaking. Noon. I sit there, frozen, staring at the screen like a battered dog waiting for a master that's never coming home.

Five minutes.

Three.

Flawed

One.

Zero.

Nothing.

Not a single message. Not a missed call. Not even a lie to hold onto.

I should move. I should breathe. I should do something. But all I can manage is to sink deeper into the couch, curled up like I'm trying to disappear inside myself. We were supposed to leave for my parents' place over an hour ago. Jax promised he'd be here. Swore up and down he wouldn't leave me hanging.

But he did.

Again.

And worse than the anger, worse than the disappointment, is the sick, hollow understanding that's been building inside me for weeks.

He was never really mine. I loved a ghost—a beautiful, flawed ghost—and it was only a matter of time before he disappeared for good. Again.

I should have known better.

I did know better.

I saw it all so clearly the first night I woke up

screaming, clutching at him like a lifeline, and he held me with hands that didn't know how to hold anything real. Jax can fake it. God, he's good at faking it. But when it comes down to it, when the ugliness leaks out, when it demands more than charm and muscle and pretty words, he's empty.

Just an echo in a handsome shell.

And me? I was stupid enough to believe if I loved him hard enough, I could fill the void.

Now I'm left bleeding out in the silence.

The phone hums softly in the background, the opening bars of 'the bitch song' playing like some cruel, ironic soundtrack. I should turn it off. I should scream. I should cry. But there's nothing left in me except numbness and a kind of grief so deep it feels like it might split me in half.

My hand shakes so badly I almost drop it.

"Hi," I rasp, shredded and raw.

"What's wrong?" Ty asks, sharp and immediate, like he can hear the damage through the line.

"I can't do it."

"What do you mean? Why?"

"I just…" My chest caves in on itself. There aren't words for this kind of hurt.

"Ally, listen to me," Ty says, slow and careful, like he's talking to a wounded animal. "Mum's not gonna pull the same shit this time. She promised. She'll call you Ally. She's gonna behave."

I let out a hollow laugh. "What'd you have to sell her for that?"

"It doesn't matter. You matter. I just want you there."

"I can't." The word shatters in my mouth. "I can't face them. I can't pretend everything's fine. I can't do this."

"Ally, you need to."

"Jax isn't coming," I whisper.

There's a long pause. When Ty speaks again, his voice is a little harder, a little more brittle.

"Come stay with me tonight. We'll go together tomorrow. You won't be alone."

I press my hand to my mouth, swallowing down the scream clawing up my throat.

"I really can't," I choke out.

The line goes deadly quiet. Then, "Hannah. Get off

your sorry arse and get in the car." His voice is tight, controlled. "If you don't, I swear to god, I will come down there and haul you out myself. I need you."

That cuts deeper than anything else could.

Ty never needs anything from me.

He's the one who gave everything. His freedom. His future. His soul. For me.

And here I am. Useless. Pathetic. Falling apart because one man walked away, when my brother has been bleeding for me for years.

I glance at the clock. 12:08.

Too late for miracles.

Too late for hope.

I force the words out, even though they taste like ash.

"I'll be there in two hours."

"It's gonna be okay, Ally," he says. "I promise."

I hang up before he can hear me sob.

I don't move for a long time. I just sit there, phone pressed to my chest, the weight of everything I've lost dragging me under.

And somewhere in the back of my mind, a small, broken voice whispers, He's not coming back.

He never was.

◆ ◆ ◆

Standing at Tyler's door feels oddly surreal.

I've never been to this apartment before, but somehow it feels more like home than the one I grew up in.

Tyler moved out the same week I did. I hadn't known Nate had been nudging him for months to move in together—Tyler stayed because of me.

Always because of me.

Always sacrificing for the sister who can't seem to get her shit together.

I knock, and the door swings open almost immediately. The place is small and a little rough around the edges, with a weird hallway smell that clings to the air. But inside, it's warm. It feels lived in. Comforting in a way that makes my throat tighten.

They were both apprentices when they moved here, now that they're both qualified mechanics, they could easily afford a bigger place, but the hassle of moving just doesn't seem worth it to them.

Tyler pulls me into a hug that's a little too tight, like he's checking to see if I'm still in one piece.

"I wasn't sure you were actually coming," he says into my hair.

"You called an hour ago. I said I was on my way."

"Yeah, but he thought you'd turn back," Nate calls from the couch, lounging in just boxers.

I force a smile. "Dressed for the occasion, I see."

"Put some clothes on," Tyler grumbles.

"She's seen me in less," Nate smirks without even blinking.

"Catching you skinny-dipping in my parents' pool isn't exactly a cherished memory," I mutter.

"Highlight of your life," he tosses over his shoulder, disappearing down the hallway.

Tyler just shakes his head, exasperated. "What happened to Mr. Perfect?"

The million-dollar question. And I don't have the energy to lie.

I shrug, even though it feels like my ribs are about to

crack from the effort of holding myself upright.

"I think it was too much for him."

"Don't be ridiculous. I've heard the way he talks about you—like you hung the goddamn moon."

"Clearly, I didn't do a very good job." The words slip out too easily, coated in self-loathing.
I don't even try to soften them.

"What did he say?" Tyler asks, his face creasing with concern.

"Nothing." I manage a brittle laugh. "He didn't have to. He just… didn't show."

A heavy pause falls between us.

"Maybe something happened—" he starts, grasping for straws, trying to put the pieces back together the way he always does.

"Nothing happened," I cut him off sharply, before doubt can take root.

Because I know better.

Because I know Jax.

Tyler stares at me, his jaw tight, the way it always gets when he's helpless to fix something.

"Well, fuck him," he says finally, voice low and

angry. "Let's get drunk."

I nod, but it feels hollow.

There's no rage left in me, no fire. Just this quiet, gnawing ache, pulling apart everything I thought we'd built.

I follow Tyler into the kitchen like a ghost trailing after a living person, and when he presses a cold beer into my hand, I barely register the chill.

I'm not here.

Not really.

I'm back on that couch, watching the clock hit noon and feeling my heart break for the last time.

I'm lying awake in bed, trying to remember what it felt like to believe someone could choose me and stay.

Tyler's talking—saying something about shots and a stupid drinking game Nate's obsessed with—but it all washes over me.

I take the shot because it's easier than feeling.

Because feeling means admitting that once again, I wasn't enough to keep him.

And I don't think I can survive knowing that.

Flawed

◆ ◆ ◆

Tyler and Nate are trying their best to get me tipsy—waving wine under my nose, daring me to do shots, bribing me with promises of greasy food and karaoke if I give in. But I'm not in the mood. I took the single shot and decide that's it. I need to stay sober. Alert. Ready for whatever family disaster might get lobbed my way like a flaming grenade.

My phone buzzed just after I arrived. Mum. Of course. Her voice was sharp enough to cut glass the moment I answered.

"So you're not coming home now? Just like that? What happened, Ally? Tyler's dirty old couch suddenly sounded more appealing than your own bed?"

She didn't need to say more. I knew the rest of the sentence—than your mother who raised you, fed you, clothed you—because she's said it a hundred times in different ways. Disappointing her used to hurt. Now it just itches. Like a scar I've learned not to scratch.

Still, it feels personal this time. Like I chose the

enemy camp.

The drive to the party was a mess of Tyler's drunken car karaoke and him and Nate bickering like two feral ten-year-olds high on red cordial. At one point, they argued for ten straight minutes over whether or not fairy bread is an acceptable adult snack. (Spoiler: it absolutely is.) I didn't say much. Just focused on driving and tried to keep my breathing steady.

But when we finally pulled up to my childhood home—the scene of a thousand tightly choreographed emotional ambushes—I froze. Just sat there in the driver's seat, keys in hand, staring blankly at the door.

Tyler circled the car and opened it gently like he was dealing with a flight risk. "Come on, Al. Deep breaths. In and out. It's only a few hours. You've got this."

He offered me a hand and a smile. I took both.

The door swung open before we even made it halfway up the path.

"You look exhausted, Ally," Mum's voice cut through the dusk like a whip. "I guess further damaging your virtue takes a toll."

There it is. The warm maternal hug I'd been

fantasising about. How silly of me.

"Nice to see you too, Mum," I muttered, forcing a smile that didn't quite reach my eyes.

She barely glanced at me before her gaze scanned the driveway.

"So where's this mysterious boyfriend? Jeanie must not be doing a great job if you're still making up stories."

Before I could summon a response that wasn't laced with every four-letter word I know, Tyler stepped in like a human shield.

"Mum, don't be a bitch. He's not imaginary—he had a work emergency. Big surprise, some people actually have lives outside this house."

Mum rolled her eyes and let out a sharp, barking laugh, like this was all one big sitcom and we were just her poorly paid supporting cast.

There's truly no place like home.

◆ ◆ ◆

Two hours in, I'm curled up beneath a tree in the backyard, hiding in the shadows.

I had dragged a wicker chair out from the patio, curling up in it like a cat looking for safety. I'd even considered slipping into the pool and sinking, but didn't want to be too dramatic.

Mum won't stop asking about my 'imaginary' boyfriend, laughing before I can answer. People stare, whisper. Tyler insists it's in my head—but this time, I know it's not.

True to his word, he stuck by me all night. Even handed me off to Nate like a security guard when he had to use the bathroom.

But I needed space. So I bolted.

Michael and Nat's parents had shown up. Despite everything, they still kept ties with my family. Another betrayal.

And when Nat arrived? Game over.

Tyler and Nat are that once-in-a-lifetime love story people write songs about. The moment she walked in, he was hers again, and I took my chance to slip away.

Alone, it hit me—Jax. His scent, his presence, even

the anger he stirred.

I hate how he still has this hold on me. Hate that I don't resent him. I replay every moment, every word, looking for signs I missed.

There were none. He left clean.

Tears sting my eyes.

Then a voice cuts through the silence.

"I was just thinking about you," he says, stepping closer with that lazy, poisonous smirk—the same one that used to slither down my spine. "I'm always thinking about you."

I can't move. Can't breathe.

It's like drowning twenty feet under, the weight of him pressing from every direction, stealing every scrap of air.

"How'd it feel?" he drawls, head cocked, eyes gleaming. "Getting everyone to swallow your little sob story?"

I force my legs to move, rising slowly, blood pounding in my ears.

What are you doing here, Michael?" my voice cracks, thin and sharp.

He shrugs, like this is just another day, another casual run-in.

"Family ties, remember? Your mum still pretends nothing ever happened. Sends out invites like she's inviting me to tea." His gaze scrapes over me, lingering. "Didn't think you'd show. Guess I'm luckier than I thought."

"Leave," I say, stiff, voice tight.

He smiles wider. Too wide. "That's no way to talk to an old friend."

"We're not friends," I bite out.

Michael's eyes gleam. Dark. Ugly.

"You sure about that?" His voice drops, thick with sick nostalgia. "You remember how close we were? How you used to laugh when I snuck you out? How you never said no when I held your hand? You liked when I touched you."

My stomach lurches.

"You liked the way I looked at you," he breathes, stepping closer. "You liked being special. Don't lie. I still remember the way you used to look at me—wide-eyed, blushing, begging for it."

"I didn't like any of it!" I snap, the words tearing out of me. "You knew exactly what you were doing."

His face hardens—just for a second—before the smirk slithers back.

"You think it wasn't good for you too?" He leans in, voice a vicious whisper. "I gave you attention when no one else did. I made you feel wanted. I made you feel alive."

I recoil like he's struck me. The memory of his hands, his breath, the way he used to corner me and twist the truth until it felt like my fault—it all crashes back.

"You should go," I say, my voice shaking but louder now. "Before Tyler sees you."

His jaw tightens, the cracks showing now, ugly and furious.

"You think he scares me?"

"I think he'd put you in the ground," I say coldly. "And no one would stop him this time."

Michael laughs—a harsh, broken sound, all teeth and rage.

"Still full of fire," he mutters. "That's what I liked best. Fighting me, crying… you were so goddamn alive under me."

My hands curl into fists at my sides, nails biting deep into my palms.

"I said leave," I growl.

"You felt so good around me," he murmurs, voice thick, eyes glazed like he's back there. "So tight. So pure."

I think I'm going to be sick.

He steps closer, lowering his voice to a sickening whisper meant only for me.

"I can make you feel good again, banana," he croons, using the name like a weapon. "I can make you moan like no one else can."

The world tilts.

The bile rises in my throat.

I taste it—the memory of him, the rot of what he did to me, what he still wants to believe.

"I didn't feel good," I choke out. "You hurt me. You broke something inside me that I'm still trying to fix."

He smiles like I just confessed something sweet.
Like my pain is a compliment.

He moves fast—too fast—reaching out like he might

grab me.

I stumble back, heart jackhammering.

"TOUCH ME AND I SWEAR TO GOD I'LL SCREAM BLOODY MURDER," I roar, loud enough to shake the air but it's drowned out by the music coming from inside the house.

He freezes—a real flicker of fear behind the rage.

Good.

"I'm not scared of you," I say, my voice trembling but true. "Not anymore. And the next time you crawl out of your hole, I'll make sure you stay buried."

Michael's face twists, teeth bared. "You think your little boyfriend's gonna save you? Heard he fucked off. Guess even he saw what a goddamn mess you are."

I don't blink. I don't flinch, no matter how much his words hurt.

"He saved me," I say, voice deadly. "From the filth you left behind."

Michael leans in one last time, a snarl behind his words.

"Just remember," he hisses. "You're not the only one with secrets. Your brother's next. And when he falls, it'll make what happened to you look like a warm-up."

Then he slinks into the dark, vanishing like the coward he's always been.

I stand there, shaking, rage and terror and hate pounding through every inch of me.

But this time, I didn't run.

My thoughts drift to Jax—not the parts that make me ache, but the quiet things. The way he looks at me like I matter. The way he believes in me, even when I didn't believe in myself.

And I realise—

I didn't find courage because I became someone else.

I found it because someone saw who I was and loved me anyway.

Jax never tried to fix me. He just loved me—fiercely, gently—and that made all the difference.

◆ ◆ ◆

When Tyler finds me twenty minutes later, I'm still trembling.

Flawed

I don't tell him what happened. I say I'm overwhelmed—by the party, by the breakup.

He doesn't push. He just wraps an arm around me, walks me through the back gate, and tells me he's proud I even came.

In the car, I lock my door instinctively. He glances at me but says nothing, calling Nate as we drive.

I cling to his arm as we head into the apartment. Only once we're inside do I finally exhale.

The adrenaline and fear crash, and I collapse onto the couch, fast asleep.

◆ ◆ ◆

The buzzing wakes me. My phone rattles on the table.

It's been three days since I left Tyler's. My apartment is my sanctuary now—home. My parents are no longer part of that equation.

I've been avoiding my bed—his scent lingers. I crash on the couch instead.

Nightmares still haunt me, but the pain is softer.

When I see the unfamiliar number, I nearly ignore it. But curiosity wins.

"Hello?" I croak.

"Ally?"

"Who is this?"

A long pause. Then, "It's Oliver."

My heart drops.

"Oh my god—is he okay?"

"Yes and no."

"What the fuck does that mean? Is he hurt?"

"No. Physically, he's fine."

Physically? That phrasing makes my skin crawl. It sounds like he's not okay mentally, which probably means this is one of those calls where a concerned family member tries to convince me that Jax is worth it despite his flaws. Well, that's not happening.

"I'm not interested in playing mind games with him. If he wants to sulk, that's on him. I'm not a preschool teacher," I retort.

Another pause. Then, finally, "Ally, he's been arrested."

The room spins.

He didn't leave?

"Why didn't he call me?" I whisper.

"He doesn't want you to know. But he's in deep shit, and he's not taking it seriously. I need you to talk some fucking sense into him."

My voice comes out barely above a breath.

"Where is he?"

CHAPTER 19

JAX

The cell is cold. The lights buzz too bright overhead, a constant reminder that time doesn't stop. But I've learned how to make it stop—for me. I've learned how to shut it all off.

That first night, her face wouldn't leave me. I feel her absence in a way I didn't think I could. Behind my eyelids—eyes wide, confused, hurt. That look she gives me when she doesn't understand. She doesn't know where I am, or why I didn't come back. I remember the way she held me like she thought I might disappear. I remember the last kiss—the one she didn't know was goodbye.

To her, I've just gone quiet.

I tell myself not to think about it. I can't.

The guilt eats at me. The urge to fix it. To explain.

But not now. I don't have the luxury.

My jaw ticks. I bark a short laugh and lean back, legs sprawled like I own the place. I've sat in interrogation rooms with blood on my knuckles and a series of charges stacked against me, and never once flinched. But this?

This silence?

It's starting to feel like it has teeth.

I rub at the back of my neck, then slam my palm flat against the wall just to hear something other than the buzzing lights. Sharp and satisfying. I do it again. Harder.

The echo is instant.

They'll think I'm agitated.

Good.

Let them.

I am.

Because I can feel her. Not in some poetic, spiritual way. No—this is visceral. Phantom-limb shit. Like she's been carved out of me and I'm walking around with the absence still bleeding.

So I shut her out. Just like that. It's easier than it should be. I've done it before—buried the feelings, pushed down the noise.

I don't do missing people. I don't need anyone. That's the whole point of the life I live. Cold. Controlled. Unattached.

She's not here. She doesn't know what's happening. All she knows is I'm not there. Worrying herself sick over what happened to me. I can picture it—her pacing the living room, checking her phone every two minutes, calling my name into the silence of a house that hasn't heard my footsteps in days. She's probably cycling through worst-case scenarios on loop, I've been hurt or I've been taken.

And the worst part? She knows.

I've told her enough times—said I love her, called her mine—enough that she can feel it in her bones. That something's happened. That something's wrong.

She just doesn't know what.

Maybe that's how I wanted it. Maybe I'm sparing her from something worse. Because she doesn't belong in this world. Not with me.

I focus on the now. The cell. The hum of the lights. The cold steel under me. Breathing through it, I force her image from my mind. If I let her in, I'll lose control.

And I can't afford that.

Tomorrow I'll be out. I'll make it right. Somehow.

But not here. Not now.

I've always been good at this. Emotions are a liability. They spread, consume, until nothing's left. I don't have room for that anymore.

One second I'm trying to remember the name of the guard's wife—because I know I fucked her once, just can't remember where or when—and the next I'm replaying the way Ally touched my jaw when she thought I was asleep. Soft. Forgiving. Like I was something worth saving.

God, I hate her for that.

Hate how she makes me feel like there's something in me worth feeling. Something breakable. Something human.

I dig my nails into my palm.

The pain helps. A bit.

Taking a deep breath and leaning back against the wall, I almost laugh. Arrested again. Of course. The charges are familiar—aggravated assault, resisting arrest, property damage. Standard fare.

The specifics were pretty standard. The police, bless their predictable socks, had followed the script I expected—handcuffs, sirens, the whole theatrical production. But this was not my first rodeo. I was well-acquainted with the routine. I made my call. Said what needed saying. By morning, I'll be out, back at her apartment, acting like none of this happened.

The government prefers it that way. Quiet. Clean. I handle their dirty work, and in return, they make things disappear.

I remind myself why I'm here. That little prick thought he had something on me. That's all this is—

nothing more. Tomorrow? I'll be out. It's all just noise. All of it. Including her.

My line of work grants me certain advantages. Let's just say the government has a vested interest in keeping things quiet—especially regarding the 'projects' I handle. A few calls and a quiet chat with a weary superior, and the charges would dissipate like mist.

I'm nearly bored, considering whether I could pick the cell lock with the paperclip I pocketed during processing. Just to see if I could. Just to prove a point.

I hear the jingle of keys and the creak of the cell door opening. The guard appears and I know that face just can't place the circumstances, but I know I've definitely fucked his wife. Judging by the tension in his jaw, so does he.

"You've got a visitor, Beckett," he says.

I raise an eyebrow. No one knows I'm here except my boss. I can't imagine he would bother coming to this dump. Ollie told me not to call next time I got nicked, so I didn't.

"All right," I say, dragging the word out. I push myself up from the cot, slow and deliberate, just to annoy him. "Let's get this circus over with."

The corridor hums with fluorescent lighting that flickers like it's trying to induce a seizure. The air reeks of disinfectant—the kind of clean that feels dirty. The visitors' room is cramped. Four walls, one table, two chairs. That's it.

I freeze in the doorway.

My fists clench. Jaw tightens. For a moment, the detachment I've built so carefully slips.

The guard nudges me forward, and I move on autopilot. Legs stiff, boots echoing across the concrete as I walk to the table.

She's already there.

Ally.

Her face—normally so full of life—is pale and drawn. Her eyes are red-rimmed, the quiet aftermath of tears she didn't want anyone to see. She looks like she hasn't slept since I left. Like I *did* this to her. Which I did.

Something twists in my chest. Guilt. My fingers twitch. I want to run. I want to reach for her. I want to kill the fucking guard for bringing her here.

"Jax," she breathes, standing as I approach. She reaches for my hands.

I pull back, stuffing mine into my pockets. The cold press of the buttons there keeps me grounded.

"It's nothing," I say. "Just a misunderstanding."

"A misunderstanding?" her voice trembles, sharper now. "Jax, the officer I spoke to said it was violent."

I shrug. "He exaggerated. Cops always do."

"But… why? Why would you break a window?"

The question hits harder than it should. I'm not ready for this part—the explanation. The exposure.

"What are you doing here?" I snap, too sharp.

She flinches. I hate myself for it. I can't stop it.

"Well?" I bite out.

"I'm sorry, Jax. It's my fault—"

"Don't give me the sob story. How the hell did you even find me?"

"Ollie called me."

"How the fuck does *he* know?"

From the corner of my eye, I catch the guard's smirk. That smug prick. He fucking lives in Ollie's building.

"You shouldn't be here, Hannah!" I shout. Her real

name slips out. Her face crumples.

"Have you contacted a lawyer?" she asks, voice small.

I let out a humourless laugh. "Don't need one."

"Jax, please. Let me help you."

I look at her, voice flat. "You want to help? Then leave. You don't want to know the things I've done. Why I'm so comfortable in here. Trust me."

Her eyes widen. "What's that supposed to mean?"

"It means you don't belong in this world. Not with me."

She looks at me like she's broken all over again, and I exhale slowly, like the tension's been holding me hostage.—sharp and bitter, laced with the kind of anger that has nowhere to go.

"I'll be out tomorrow," I add, deadpan. "This is just theatre. That little prick thinks he's got something on me."

"Jax, this is serious. You're in real trouble."

"Why are you even here?" I snap, louder than I mean to. I'm not supposed to *feel* anything. Not here. But with her standing in front of me—eyes red, voice trembling

—I feel *everything*.

She doesn't answer.

"Stop crying," I say, softer this time. The fight drains out of me in an instant. "I'll be back at your place tomorrow."

"What?" Her voice is barely audible.

"I'll be home tomorrow."

She blinks, confused, vulnerable in a way that guts me. "I… I thought you ran again," she whispers.

Fuck.

The world tilts on its axis. I was so caught up in the fallout—so deep in the rage and the aftermath—I didn't even think about how it would affect her but her insecurities are written all over her face.

I reach for her. She pulls away.

"I was trying to protect you," I say. All the bravado gone.

"By disappearing again? Not calling? I've cried myself to sleep for four days, Jax. Four fucking days."

Again.

She thinks I left her again.

The wall I built around myself cracks. Falls.

"You belong to me, Ally. I'll never abandon you again. I'd rather watch the world burn than walk away from you."

She stares at me. "So now I'm Ally again? Why *are* you so comfortable in here?"

Well, fuck.

I shrug. "I mentioned I work for the government?"

"Yeah, so?"

"I took the job in exchange for not serving serious time."

She opens her mouth to speak but closes it, repeating the motion, as if the words won't come. "What... what did you do?" she asks cautiously, her voice trembling with uncertainty.

"Turns out the Australian Defence Force doesn't appreciate it when you hack their system repeatedly."

"Why the fuck would you hack the defence force?!"

"Keep your voice down." I hiss, glaring at her.

"More than once?"

"Their IT was shit. It was fun. They redesigned it—I broke in again. Eventually, they offered me a job."

"You need fucking medication," she snaps.

I laugh. Can't help it.

"Seriously, Jax! You're fucking psychotic."

"Yeah, we've established that," I add with an eye roll. "Anyway, they offered me a job to redesign their system so people like me couldn't get in, in exchange for not serving 20 plus years. It also pays really well, so I figured why not?"

She stares at me, mouth hanging open in disbelief.

"I did tell you I'm very good at what I do," I add with a small smile, trying to lighten the mood.

"It still doesn't explain how it helps you now though."

"Perks of the job. I'm valuable. They won't risk losing me. That cunt just thinks he's got something on me because I've got a record."

She pauses, eyes narrowing. "That's how he knew you weren't around. He knew you'd been arrested."

"Times up, Beckett," the guard calls out. But I'm too focused on what she just said—my blood running cold in my veins.

"What did you just say?" I hiss.

"Michael was at my parents' on Saturday. He knew

you weren't with me."

"You went home Saturday?"

Before I know it, I'm on my feet. The chair screeches back as I stand. I grab the edge of the table and hurl it across the room.

He was there. He got close to her. Spoke to her.

She wasn't supposed to leave. She was supposed to be safe.

My chest heaves with the realisation—I wasn't there. I shut her out. I thought she was safe.

Two guards storm in, dragging me back before I can get another word out. Before I can make sure she's okay.

CHAPTER 20

ALLY

I look around the room, completely dazed. I still don't know how I ended up here. One minute I was leaving the correctional centre, my chest tight, my head full of Jax's voice and the way he'd looked at me like he wanted me gone. The next, I was sitting outside Ty's apartment, the engine off, my hands clenched so tight around the steering wheel they'd gone numb.

His car was out front, so I knew he was home. But I couldn't bring myself to get out. Couldn't move. I just sat there, eyes fixed on his front door like it might open and give me an answer. Something. Anything. Instead, time passed, slow and heavy. My breath fogged up the windscreen. I didn't even wipe it away.

It wasn't until Nate pulled up on his lunch break that I snapped out of it. He parked beside me, cut the engine, and knocked on my window like he was scared he would frighten me if I wasn't handled gently. I must've looked wrecked because he didn't ask a single question. He just opened the door, took my keys, and helped me inside. Like he'd done it a hundred times before. Like this wasn't the first time I'd fallen apart.

He banged on Ty's door with his usual dramatic flair, told him I was here, and then—without waiting for an answer—he grabbed his gym bag and headed back to work.

I haven't seen Ty yet. Apparently, he called in sick after drinking too much last night, which tracks. The man handles his feelings with alcohol the way most people use Panadol. The clock on the wall reads 1PM, and I can't sit still anymore. I need to talk. Or scream. Or cry. I just need something.

I creep down the hallway and push open his bedroom door without knocking, like I used to when we were kids and I needed comfort after a nightmare. But this—this is a nightmare of a different kind.

Ty's curled up in bed, shirtless, looking predictably like roadkill. But it's not him that stops me dead in my tracks.

It's her.

Natalie.

Naked, tangled in his sheets, her signature deep red hair spread out across his pillow like a warning sign. I stand there, rooted to the spot, my brain short-circuiting as I try to process this reality. My jaw practically hits the floor. I freeze, one foot still hovering in the air, and everything just… stops. It's almost too much to handle—almost as much of a shock as the mess with Jax.

I back out of the room and quietly close the door behind me. I can't deal with this right now. I pace around the kitchen, my mind a mess, before deciding I need to get the fuck out of here. Nate knows I'm here, and there will be questions, but I'd rather have that conversation hiding behind my phone.

I reach for the door handle just as a sleepy voice stops me.

"Banana?"

My spine goes rigid. The nickname wraps around me like barbed wire.

"Don't call me that," I snap, sharper than I mean to. I don't even look at her.

A moment later, Ty's voice cuts through, "It's Ally."

I can hear the shift in him. The tension.

"What are you doing here?" he asks, and there's a bite to it. Defensive.

I don't turn around. My hand is still on the door. "I'm sorry. I didn't mean to… I'm leaving."

He moves fast. I hear the soft tread of his feet across the floor and then feel his hand close around my wrist. Not hard. Just enough to stop me.

"Ally. What's going on?"

I finally turn to face him. His eyes are bloodshot, hair a mess, shirtless, the waistband of his trackies hanging low. He's trying to put on a brave face, but I see the guilt flash behind his eyes. Natalie hovers behind him now, wearing one of his oversized shirts. She looks embarrassed. Awkward.

"I… I just needed somewhere to go," I say weakly. "I'm sorry, I didn't mean to intrude. I didn't see anything. I'm leaving."

"I'm gonna go. I'll let you two talk," Natalie mutters, clearly uncomfortable, as she heads off in search of her clothes.

"Fuck," Ty mutters under his breath. "Just give me a minute." He follows her out of the room. I don't move. I just stand there, arms wrapped around my middle like they're the only thing holding me together.

Ty comes back five minutes later—Nat fully dressed, Ty now in a shirt. He walks her to the door, and to my surprise, he takes her hand before telling me he's walking her to her car.

When he comes back, he walks straight past me, grabs the tequila bottle from the freezer—because DNA is strong like that—and holds it out.

I don't hesitate.

He flops down onto the couch beside me and takes a long swig. Then passes it back.

"So…" he says eventually. "You gonna tell me what's going on?"

I take a sip, let the burn settle in my chest. "You first."

He raises an eyebrow. "You mean Nat?"

I nod.

He groans and leans back. "Ran into her at The Gully last night. One drink turned into five, and then…" He shrugs. "It just happened."

"And this wasn't a thing before?"

He gives me a look. "No. Not for years."

I sigh. "I'm not mad."

He laughs, disbelieving.

"I'm not. I just… it's not the news I needed today."

"Yeah, well. Welcome to the club."

We sit in silence for a moment, the tequila bottle between us.

"Jax got arrested," I say suddenly. The words drop like a stone.

Ty blinks. "What?"

"That's why he didn't come home. Why he went quiet. He didn't want me to know."

Ty laughs, shaking his head. "Can't say I blame him. You tend to overreact. Remember how you carried on when I got arrested? And that's just the time you know about."

"What the fuck!" I stare at him, pissed, but also a little too overwhelmed to keep my composure. Ty doesn't get it—he doesn't know Jax has disappeared on me before. Of course he can brush it off.

Ty frowns. "What happens now?"

I shake my head. "He says it's nothing. Just a misunderstanding. But he smashed a window while getting arrested. It sounded bad."

Ty whistles low. "You sure know how to pick 'em."

I glare at him. "Don't."

He holds up his hands in surrender. "Sorry. Just… wow"

"Yeah. Tell me about it."

He watches me, his expression softening. "You okay?"

I don't answer straight away. Because no, I'm not.

I'm a mess. My heart feels like it's been scraped raw. I don't know where I stand with Jax. I don't even know where I stand with myself.

"I don't know," I whisper.

Ty shifts closer, throws an arm over my shoulders, and pulls me in like he used to when I was little.

"You're always welcome here," he murmurs. "No questions asked."

I lean into him, resting my head on his shoulder. We sit like that for a long time, passing the tequila back and forth, watching trash TV with the volume too low to hear.

By the time Nate gets home, the bottle is empty, the daylight has faded, and we're both pretending—just for now—that nothing's wrong.

CHAPTER 21

JAX

It takes that motherfucker I work for another twenty-four hours to get me out of that shithole. A slap on the wrist and a week off work unpaid. That's what breaking a predator's jaw gets me. Lucky me.

But I'm losing my mind.

I can't disconnect from the shit running laps in my

head. Not when Ally is the only thing I can think about. Not after finding out she wasn't safe at home like I thought she was. I pictured her curled up in our bed, scrolling through her phone, waiting on my call.

Instead, she was facing her demons without me.

She's stronger than I give her credit for. Leaving the city. Confronting the parents who broke her. And doing it alone.

The second I'm out, I don't even go home. I throw myself into a cab and tell the driver to take me to her apartment. I don't care how I look, or what time it is. I just need to see her.

The doorman—a frumpy bastard who's always hated my guts—barely looks up when I walk in.

"She's not home," he mutters before I can even ask. No apology. No warmth.

I've called her a dozen times since I left the station. Nothing. Radio silence.

I try to sit in the lobby, but I last nine seconds before I'm pacing like a caged animal. My fists clench and unclench at my sides. My jaw is so tight I'm seconds from cracking a molar.

Thirty more minutes pass. Still no answer. Still no sign of her.

Finally, the concierge strolls over, smug as hell.

"She didn't come home last night," he says, like he's just remembered.

"You're telling me now?" I step in, towering over him. "What the fuck have I been sitting here for?"

He shrinks back a little, and I have to talk myself down. I can't afford to get arrested again.

Where the fuck is she?

I force myself to breathe. Think. I need something. A lead. A trail.

"I need to use your computer," I snap.

He stares at me. "Excuse me?"

"It's important," I grit out. "She might be hurt."

He hesitates, but then sighs. "Only because I care about Ally."

I'm in her email within seconds. I search everything. Inbox, outbox, drafts. Nothing helpful. Just a string of emails to Jeanie, scheduling phone calls. My chest aches. She's been struggling and I wasn't there.

"She gave you her password?" he asks, skeptical.

"She sure did."

When I hit a wall, I slam the keyboard harder than I should. The guy jumps, eyes wide.

Fucking pussy.

"You try her emergency contact?" he mutters. It hits me like a freight train.

It's not me.

"Who the fuck is her emergency contact?" I growl.

The prick looks at me like I've lost my mind before responding, "I can't give you that information."

I push the jealousy aside long enough for my rational brain to kick in.

I yank out my phone and dial.

It rings twice before a voice picks up— calm like he was just waiting for my call

"Yeah, she's here."

Relief. A burst of air fills my lungs. She's safe.

But not with me.

"She's not answering her phone."

"She left it here. Went out. Needed a break."

"You let her go?" I explode. "Are you fucking insane?!"

"She's a big girl, Jax."

"Where is she?"

"I'm obviously missing a lot here, but if she wanted you to know, she'd have told you."

"You stupid cunt!" I yell, loud enough that Paul the Prick gives me a horrified look.

"I'll tell her to call you," Tyler says, like he's the reasonable one here. "I'm rooting for you. Really." Click.

Fucking *asshole*.

I storm back to the desk, ignoring Paul's protests. One quick search through Ally's sent items gives me Tyler's email. Another sixty seconds and I've hacked in. I'm not even trying to be subtle. His most recent payslip is sitting right there.

Residential address: locked and loaded.

I snap a photo of the screen and—because I'm petty —I change his email password on the way out.

When I turn around, Paul's staring at me like I've grown horns.

"Remind me never to piss you off."

I grin and slap his back. "Glad we understand each

other."

Then I'm gone.

I flag a cab and tell the driver the address. He blinks like I've lost my mind. *What is it with people thinking I'm crazy today?*

Money talks so I offer him a thousand dollar tip if he gets me there fast. When you move through life without a conscience, it's easy to win. No guilt, no hesitation— just strategy. That kind of cold efficiency tends to pay off, and my bank account proves it.

Two hours later, we pull up. It's late afternoon, sun casting long shadows, and I'm already halfway out of the car before it fully stops.

No sign of her car.

Shit.

I run up the stairs and pound on the door. The annoying friend with the ridiculous mohawk opens it, leaning against the frame like this is some kind of joke.

"Hey, boyfriend. 'Bout time you showed up."

"Where is she?"

"She's not back yet. Won't be long."

I rake my hands through my hair, pacing the hallway.

"I swear, if that cunt goes near her again, I'll kill him."

"What cunt?" another voice cuts in. Tyler, stepping out of the hallway.

"How do you even know where I live?" he adds skeptically.

"The cunt with the broken jaw," I snap, eyes burning. "I'll skin him alive. Then I'll come back here and kill both of you idiots for letting her out of your sight."

Tyler stiffens. Nate swears under his breath.

The tension thickens—coiled and electric—until the front door creaks open behind me.

I turn.

And there she is.

She looks… wrecked. Pale. Hollowed out. But still the most breathtaking thing I've ever seen.

I don't even think.

I cross the room and lift her into my arms. Her body melts into mine like she was made to fit there. I bury my face in her neck, breathing her in. Vanilla and warmth and home.

"You found me," she whispers.

"I'll always find you," I rasp. And I mean it. Every fucking word.

I'd drown the stars and salt the sky if it meant she stayed untouched by the things that haunt her.

Her fingers curl into the back of my shirt, like she's afraid I'll disappear if she lets go. I hold her tighter, feeling the frantic beat of her heart against my chest, matching the rhythm of my own.

"You're safe," I murmur against her skin. "You're mine."

She pulls back just enough to look up at me, her eyes glassy and shining, a lifetime of fear and hope tangled in one look. It guts me—the way she trusts me to hold it all without dropping a single piece.

"You promise?" she asks, voice cracking.

I brush my thumb across her cheek, catching a tear before it can fall.

"With every fucked-up piece of me," I swear.

And it's not some shiny vow made in a perfect world. It's messy and broken and real the only kind of promise I know how to give.

Her mouth finds mine, desperate and searching. I kiss

her back like a man starved, because I am—starved for her, for the taste of something good in a world that's done nothing but rot.

Someone clears their throat, and for a moment, I'd forgotten we weren't alone.

She pulls back, cheeks flushing pink as she turns to her brother.

"Thanks for letting me hide out here," she says, trying to gather herself.

He watches us for a beat, something unreadable flickering in his eyes, before he says,

"Door's always open. But Jax, if she ever shows up on my doorstep in tears again, I'm coming after you."

My first instinct is to remind him that I still want to lay him out for that gay comment debacle, but I bite it back.

Because the truth is, he's the only other person on this planet who'd go almost as far as I would for Ally.

He loves her. Wants what is best for her. And he's smart enough to know sometimes the thing she needs protecting from is me.

I guess that makes us allies, in a fucked-up way.

So instead of swinging, I nod once—sharp, certain. "That won't be necessary," I tell him.

Then I take my girl's hand and drag her out the door, not planning to let go anytime soon.

◆ ◆ ◆

We don't go back to the apartment.

I take her to the nearest hotel and don't let her go the entire ride.

When the door shuts behind us, I hold her like I'm afraid she'll disappear. It's not about sex. It's not about control. It's about needing her close, needing to feel her heart beating against mine to believe she's really here.

She doesn't pull away. Just wraps her arms around my neck and lets me hold her like she belongs there.

And she does.

In my arms. In my world.

Mine.

Always.

CHAPTER 22

ALLY

He pulls away slightly, his hands still cup my face, thumbs brushing softly over my cheeks like I might dissolve if he's not careful. There's something in his eyes I don't think I've ever seen before—fear, maybe. Not of me, but of losing me. It's like he's memorising every part of me in case I disappear.

I thread my fingers through his, grounding myself in his touch. When I take a cautious step back, he follows instantly, silent, relentless—until the backs of my knees brush the edge of the bed. His body doesn't touch mine, not yet, but I can feel the weight of his presence pressing into every inch of my skin.

"I missed you, beautiful," he murmurs, voice barely a whisper, his lips brushing mine in a kiss so soft it almost hurts. There's reverence in it. Like he's kissing something holy.

I melt into him. I part my lips, seeking more, and he gives it—just enough. Just enough to make my lungs forget how to work.

My hands slide beneath the hem of his shirt and lift it over his head. He doesn't rush me. Doesn't push. Instead, he tucks a loose strand of hair behind my ear and presses another kiss to my mouth—deeper this time, but still unhurried, like he's trying to pour something into me. Like he's trying to say everything without words.

When I strip off my shirt and bra, he just looks at me. His gaze flicks between my eyes and my chest as if he's not sure where to settle. When his hands find my breasts, his touch is gentle. Worshipful. His thumbs brush softly over my nipples before his mouth replaces them, warm and wet and slow, like he's trying to rewrite the way I remember being touched.

A soft moan escapes me as I arch into him. I undo his jeans, watching his eyes darken with each inch of skin I expose. But still, he waits. He lets me set the pace, lets me turn him back toward the bed until the back of his knees hit the edge and I push him gently down. I undress slowly, aware of his eyes tracking every movement. There's nothing ravenous about it, but the hunger is there—controlled. Contained. Just barely.

I climb into his lap, straddling him, and trail kisses along his throat, feeling the rasp of stubble graze my lips. When I reach his mouth again, he meets me with a kiss that is all emotion—no game, no control, no darkness—just him.

"I need you, Ally," he breathes, his voice gravelly and vulnerable. "I need to feel you. I need to know you're mine."

His hands explore me like they've forgotten how I

feel—gliding down my waist, over my hips, then gripping my ass to bring me flush against him. His cock presses against my stomach, hard and heavy, but he doesn't act on it—not yet.

"You're so fucking beautiful," he murmurs against my throat, reverent and almost broken. He lifts me effortlessly, easing me onto the bed like I'm something delicate. Something irreplaceable.

"I need to taste you," he whispers.

He kisses his way down my body, slow and deliberate, leaving behind a trail of heat. When he spreads my thighs, his gaze lingers—hungry, possessive, and yet, tender.

The first stroke of his tongue makes my hips jerk, a gasp ripping from my chest. His mouth is relentless but careful, fingers working in perfect rhythm with his tongue as he drags me to the edge.

"Come for me," he growls, the darkness slipping through now, like smoke under a door. "I need to feel you fall apart on my tongue."

His voice alone sends me spiralling. I cry out, my body arching as pleasure overtakes me, his tongue coaxing every last tremor from me before he finally pulls away.

He hovers over me, eyes wild and dark with want. His cock is thick and hard against my thigh, and when I reach for him, he groans, hips twitching forward into my grasp. But before I can guide him further, he wraps his hand around my wrist and brings it to his lips to press a kiss to the inside of it.

Then he shifts, positioning himself between my thighs. The tip of his cock slides against me, and I wrap my legs around his waist, pulling him in.

He threads our fingers together again and holds my gaze as he pushes inside me—slow, careful, inch by inch, until he's fully seated.

And then he stills.

His eyes never leave mine. He doesn't move. He just stays there, buried deep, his breath ragged, his heart pounding against my chest.

It's intimate. Painfully so. This isn't the man who fucks me like he owns me. This is the man who needs to believe he still has a soul.

When he begins to move, it's slow. Intoxicating.

Every stroke drags against my inner walls in a way that has me gasping for air, clinging to him. It's almost too much. The intimacy, the pressure, the tenderness wrapped around something so primal.

"Fuck, Ally," he breathes, the edge of darkness curling back in. "You feel so fucking good. I could die right here."

His pace quickens just enough to push me over again when his fingers find my clit, stroking in time with his thrusts.

We come together—his name tumbling from my lips as my body convulses around him. He groans, burying his face in my neck as he empties himself inside me, his body trembling.

He collapses on top of me, breaths hot against my skin, whispering things I don't fully catch—but they sound like love, and want, and desperate need.

And for now, none of it scares me.

We lie tangled together, our hearts finally beat in rhythm. For the first time, I don't feel adrift. I don't feel like something broken. I feel claimed. Held. Loved.

"I love you, Ally," Jax whispers, sleep clinging to his

voice. "And I swear, I'll keep you safe. Always."

"I believe you," I whisper back, letting the weight of his words carry me into sleep.

◆ ◆ ◆

The first thing I notice when I wake up is the stillness. Waking usually feels like bracing for impact— a jolt from some lingering nightmare or the weight of everything waiting on the other side of consciousness. But not today. The fog of sleep lifts slowly, like the world is exhaling around me. There's no panic, no tension in my chest. Just quiet. Just light, soft and pale, slipping through the cracks in the curtains and casting faint patterns across the floor.

The room is cool, but the air smells faintly of sandalwood—and him. Jax. I can feel his presence behind me, warm and solid, his arm resting protectively across my waist. His breathing is slow, steady. Peaceful. Real.

I shift slightly, careful not to break the moment, but needing to know—needing to be sure this isn't a dream.

That this, him holding me, this stillness, is really happening. His arm tightens around me just enough to draw me closer, and his voice—low and rough with sleep—brushes against my ear.

"Ally?" he mumbles, half-awake.

"I'm here," my voice barely makes a sound, but he hears it. His grip softens, like it's enough just to know I haven't disappeared.

"Are you okay?" There's a crack in his voice that undoes me a little. Something fragile and real.

"I'm okay," I say, surprised by how calm I sound when my insides are still twisted up.

"I was so scared," he murmurs. "I went to your place and they told me you hadn't come home the other night. And then Tyler wouldn't tell me where you were, and I just—" he pauses, his breath catching, and I feel the tension rising in his body—"I thought something had happened to you. I thought I was gonna end up in jail for murder. I couldn't breathe, Ally."

He pulls me tighter, his arm around me like a shield. And there it is, the reason for his quiet intensity, the way he made love to me last night like I was something fragile. The fear. The not knowing.

I don't say anything for a while. Just let my body sink into his, my head resting on his chest, letting the rhythm of his breathing calm the mess inside me. His hand starts stroking my hair, slow and gentle, like he needs the contact just as much as I do.

"I went to the police station yesterday," I say quietly. "After I saw Jeanie."

I feel him tense underneath me instantly.

"Why? What did he—?"

"Nothing," I cut him off before the anger fully rises. "Nothing new. I reported the attack in the parking lot. The one you already know about."

He goes quiet, but the tension stays. I can feel it simmering under his skin.

"Why did you do that?" he asks finally, voice low and sharp at the edges.

I take a breath. "So there's a record," I say. "So what you did doesn't look like some random act of violence. It was retaliation. He deserved it."

His body slowly starts to relax against mine, like the weight of it finally lifts. He exhales, the sound heavy.

"You didn't have to do that for me," he says softly. "I told you it'd be okay."

"I didn't just do it for you," I whisper. "I needed to do it for me, too. I should've reported him the first time. I never should've let it get that far. And… I got an AVO. He's not allowed near me again."

"You never told me what happened at your parents' place."

I give him the short version, but he's not having it— he wants every detail.

He's quiet for a second. Then I feel his arms wrap tighter around me, like he wants to shield me from everything.

"I'm proud of you," he says, so softly it hurts. "That must've been so fucking hard. You shouldn't have had to do that alone."

"I wanted to," I say, shifting just enough to look up at him. "I needed to. I had to prove to myself that I could do it on my own."

His gaze softens, but I can still see the frustration lingering there.

"That's why your brother wouldn't tell me where you

were," he mutters. "Jesus, Ally, I nearly knocked his fucking teeth out."

I can't help it—I laugh. It's small, but real. And after everything, it feels like a miracle.

"You're not as scary as you think you are."

He smacks my ass, making me yelp in surprise, and I burst into full laughter.

"Hey!" I say, still laughing as the tension fades into something lighter. "That's not fair."

"Maybe next time you'll listen to me when I tell you to stay safe," he says, teasing but still deadly serious underneath it.

Silence settles between us again, but it's the good kind of quiet. I stretch a little, melting into his warmth.

"So," he says eventually, voice low and a little mischievous. "What are we doing today?"

I tilt my head back, caught off guard by the question. "I just want to go home," I murmur, thinking about familiar walls and quiet mornings. I just want to feel safe again.

He shakes his head, a smirk tugging at his lips. "Fuck that. I want to meet Mummy Dearest."

I freeze, whipping my head toward him, eyebrows raised. "Why the fuck would you want that?"

He leans in, presses a slow kiss to my forehead. "Because anyone who makes you sad has to go through me."

My heart stutters. Of course he'd say something like that. Of course he'd mean it.

I let out a shaky breath and look up at him again. "Hey can I ask you something?"

Another kiss, this one on my shoulder. His hand slides lazily up my arm, fingers drawing soft shapes.

"Anything, beautiful."

I hesitate. "Did you… move in with me?"

He laughs quietly, the sound vibrating against my back. "Yeah. We talked about it."

I blink. *We did?* I search my memory, trying to grasp at the fragment of the conversation he's referring to, but nothing comes to mind. I look at him, furrowing my brow in confusion.

"We did?" I ask, my voice thick with doubt.

He chuckles again, a low rumble that makes my heart skip a beat. "You were asleep at the time," he explains, his thumb tracing the line of my jaw as if he's trying to soothe away the confusion. "I was afraid you'd say no, so I just, uh… kept it casual. But we definitely had the conversation. It was riveting."

I roll my eyes, but I can't stop the smile spreading across my face. "Do you want to live with me, Jackson?"

He studies me for a beat, and then his voice turns soft, serious. "I do, Ally. I'll rent my place out and move in. But this time, you'll be awake when we talk about it."

I sit up a little. "Wait—your place? You own it?"

He just shrugs, that same unreadable little smile on his face. "Bought it last year. But let's not get into the details of that right now."

I open my mouth to ask something else, but I stop myself. It doesn't matter right now. Not really. What matters is that he's here. Holding me. That he wants to stay.

I settle back into his chest, letting my eyes fall shut. His warmth. His breath. His heartbeat. That's all I need for now.

Peace.

◆ ◆ ◆

The knot in my stomach tightens with every kilometre we drive toward my parents' place. Jax—bless his oblivious heart—hums along to the radio, completely unaware of the disaster waiting for him.

Bringing him here to meet my parents is a terrible idea. Scratch that, it's a fucking disastrous idea. I'm trying to convince myself that if anyone can handle my mum, it's Jax. And maybe, just maybe, she'll be on her best behaviour.

God I'm delusional.

"So, your mum's a university lecturer, huh?" Jax asks, shooting me a grin. "What does she teach?"

"Religious studies," I mumble, staring out the window. "She's very… polished."

Polished is one word for it. Condescending, judgy, and emotionally exhausting are others that come to mind. Mum's not just a hardarse—she's a walking, talking archive of every mistake I've ever made. From my teenage fashion disasters to my so-called life choices, she's got the full file, colour-coded and ready to go.

We pull into the driveway of their perfect, smug-looking house, the kind that screams, 'I have a designer herb garden and my daughter needs therapy.' I quickly text Tyler an SOS, not even bothering to pretend I'm happy to be here.

Jax, picking up on my nerves, gives my thigh a squeeze and tips my chin up to meet his eyes.

"Come on, this'll be fun."

"Jax…" I groan, dreading what's about to unfold.

"I know, I know. Best behaviour. Fireman Sam reporting for duty." He winks, grinning like a kid on Christmas as he jumps out and comes around to open my door.

I take a deep breath.

The second the front door to the house opens, the air drops ten degrees. My mum greets us with a smile so tight it could crack glass.

"Ally, you're here. And this must be Jax," she says, holding out a hand like she's about to interview him.

"Lovely to finally meet you. I was starting to think you made him up. You're definitely not what I expected."

Ouch. I wince and glance at Jax, bracing for impact.

But he doesn't miss a beat.

"Pleasure's mine," he says smoothly." I assure you, I'm very real—and even better when you get the hands-on experience."

I nearly choke. Jesus, he's already dropped an innuendo, and we've only just stepped over the threshold.

Mum clears her throat, clearly unsure whether to be scandalised or just confused.

"Hannah can be a lot of work, I'm sure you have your hands full."

"Not at all, *Ally* is a delight. Although, I find that the tighter the situation, the more satisfying it is when you finally slip through. You see, it's all about fit, Mrs. Barlowe, and trust me, once I find a good, tight fit... I don't let go easily."

"Where's Dad?" I ask, trying to break the awkward energy.

"Out back. Go on through. I'll make some tea. Jax,

like one?"

"I'd love one."

"How do you take it?"

"Doesn't matter, just as long as Ally blows it for me," he adds, deadpan.

I burst out laughing. I can't help it. The way my mum's face freezes mid-turn is almost too much. I grab Jax's hand and drag him down the hall before she can regain the power of speech.

"You're awful," I hiss, grinning.

"What? I love a good cup of tea," he says innocently.

"I don't hate my dad," I warn as we reach the backyard.

"Noted," he replies, his tone dripping with fake seriousness.

"Hey, Dad," I call.

"Han—Ally. What are you doing here?" Dad stammers, clearly flustered by my unexpected visit.

"Dad, this is Jax."

"Pleasure to meet you, Mr. Barlowe," Jax says, shaking his hand. "Ally's spoken so highly of you."

My dad raises an eyebrow but shakes his hand

anyway. "That's hard to believe, but I appreciate your assumption."

"I hope I'm not overstepping," Jax continues. "But you've raised an incredible daughter. She's strong, kind, beautiful. She's everything to me, and I'll look after her with everything I have."

My heart actually aches. It's not just what he says—it's how he says it. With absolute conviction.

"Well, Jax, that's not too forward at all. You seem like a nice young man. And Ally looks happy. That's what matters."

Mum strolls out just as we're sitting down at the outdoor table.

"So, Jax," she says, all fake-casual charm. "What do you do for work?"

She's wearing that smug little smile, clearly expecting him to say something without formal education—manual labour, maybe security at a shopping centre.

"I'm in IT. I'm a senior programmer for the Australian Defence Force, specialising in international cybersecurity and the protection of virtual data."

I try to school my expression, but it's no use. My mouth falls open in surprise. I know what Jax does for a living, but hearing the title? Damn, it's downright impressive. Jax gently lifts my chin, closing my slack jaw, and I realise my eyes have probably gone as wide as my shock. Not only is he sexy as hell, but his ability to shut my mother up is fucking doing things to me.

We last maybe forty-five peaceful minutes. It's almost frightening how quickly Jax can flip the switch. He'd been all charm in front of my dad, offering to help my mum clean up the tea cups and biscuits. But the moment the three of us step into the kitchen, he makes a comment about how 'tight' my mum has her porcelain 'pussy' cat salt and pepper shakers arranged. "Haven't seen pussies that tight since year twelve formal."

I almost wet myself laughing. Mum nearly drops the teapot.

Ty walks in just as I'm wheezing.

"Fuck, Ally. Haven't heard you laugh like that in years," he says, giving me a hug.

"Oh, Tyler, sweetheart," Mum says, all sweet and lovingly. "Ran into Natalie at the shops. Told her you said hi. Such a lovely girl. Shame your sister had to ruin that for you."

I freeze. The tension snaps through me like a whip.

But it's Jax who moves first.

"Alright," he says, too calm. The kind of calm that makes your skin crawl. "Enough with the dog and pony show. What the actual fuck is wrong with you?"

"Jax—" I try, already knowing it's too late.

"No. I'm not holding my tongue for her. She's a cunt and if she opens her mouth like that again, I'll make sure she chokes on it. I don't give a shit if she's your mother —no one talks to you like that. Not in front of me. Not ever."

His eyes don't leave hers. Ice-cold. Unblinking.

"We're done here, Ally. Grab your stuff. We're going home. Our home. Because this?" He gestures to the room. "This isn't home."

Mum lets out a bitter, mocking laugh. "Living in sin, too? Where did I go so wrong with you?"

"Oh, you want to talk *wrong*?" Jax snaps, his smile sudden and terrifying. "Say one more word, and I'll make sure every university board in the state gets a nice little leak from your files. Passwords only keep secrets until someone like me gets bored."

Her face drains of colour.

Jax leans in, smiling like the devil himself. "Glad we understand each other."

He takes my hand and starts walking. As we pass Tyler, Jax says over his shoulder, "Sorry for calling *your* mum a cunt, but she kind of is."

Ty shrugs. "Don't worry about it. I've been telling her in a more pleasant way for years."

"Fuck pleasantries," Jax says loudly, his voice echoing as we exit the house.

The moment we step outside, the tears start to fall, and I can't even begin to stop them. Relief, shock, something like elation—the last five days slamming into me at once, so hard it leaves me shaking, barely able to stay upright.

I fall into him, but for once, it's not from being *broken*. It feels like release.

Jax notices before I can hide it. He doesn't hesitate. He pulls off his jacket and wraps it around me, but it's not the cold he's shielding me from—he knows it. His hands linger, firm and steady, holding me together when I feel like I might shatter into pieces right there on the sidewalk.

His jacket smells like him—woodsy, soap, heat—and the familiar weight of it around my shoulders makes the dam inside me finally break. A broken sob escapes before I can swallow it down.

"Hey, hey, it's okay," Jax mutters, his voice low and rough, more a vow than a comfort. His arms stay around me, strong and certain, as if he could physically hold all my broken pieces in place if he just tried hard enough.

I burrow into him without thinking, desperate for the safety he offers, desperate for him.

And he just holds me tighter, like letting go isn't even an option.

As I pull myself together, he opens the car door, settles me in, then gets behind the wheel and backs out of the driveway.

We drive in easy silence for a few minutes before he says, "I'm sorry."

He's not—and we both know it.

"Don't apologise. Do you really have something on

her?"

"Never go into battle unprepared, beautiful," he says, smirking.

"Do I want to know?"

"Probably not."

"That was genuinely the highlight of my life," I say. "You might finally get that thing you've been begging for."

He perks up. "You're going to let me fuck your arse?"

"I think you've earned it." He shakes his head, as if trying to clear the visual of thoughts in his mind.

"Then why are you crying, beautiful?" he asks gently.

"I'm just… relieved. She's bullied me for years, and someone finally stood up to her."

"She had it coming," he mutters.

I settle into the seat, heart still thudding, body trembling.

Jax flicks the blinker. "Quick detour before we hit the freeway."

"Where to?" I ask, frowning.

"Just need to say a quick hello to someone," he says,

already pulling over.

Before I can ask more, he's out the door.

"Stay here, beautiful. I won't be long."

CHAPTER 23

JAX

I'm on a fucking warpath. My vision tunnels, blood pumps hot through my veins as I push through the doors of the seedy bar, swallowed by dim lighting and the heavy, musky air.

Keep your shit together. Keep your shit together. The mantra loops in my head like a broken record.

I will not lose my shit.

Flawed

Most people are creatures of habit. It's amazing what you can dig up on someone just by skimming through their bank statements—their movements, their routine, the sleazy pubs where they grab lunch. Details like that.

I scan the room and spot the piece of shit sitting at the bar, leering at the bartender—a petite woman with brunette hair.

He has a type. Interesting

I stride over and slide into the seat next to him. The bar's nearly empty, so my movement snags his attention instantly. His head snaps toward me, and I watch the shift—predator to prey. His posture tightens, a quick breath hitches in his throat.

Good. He should be scared.

"What can I get you, handsome?" the bartender purrs, giving me a once-over.

"Nothing, thanks," I say, not looking at her. "I won't be staying."

The jizzstain flinches at the sound of my voice, and a dark thrill crackles through me.

"You know," I say, low and casual, "I've been thinking about you. A lot."

"How did you—?"

I don't let him finish.

"You went near her. Spoke to her. Tried to scare her."

He turns toward me, glaring, trying to wear his bravado like armour. But it's thin. His fear leaks through his eyes.

"I'm going to make this really simple," I say, my tone calm—almost gentle—but laced with steel. "I'm not the law. I don't play by rules. And when it comes to protecting her, I've got nothing to lose. So think real hard before you fuck with me."

He opens his mouth like he wants to fire back, but I keep going.

"Stay away from her. Don't call. Don't show your face. Don't even think of her name. Because if you do, I will castrate you and use your genitals as a ball gag to keep you quiet while I skin you alive and cut you into pieces so small there won't be enough left to bury."

"You sound like a fucking psycho," he spits, clinging to his facade—and failing miserably.

"Don't let the 'high-functioning' fool you." I smile. "I'm the real deal, shit stain. And I'll be whoever I need to be to make sure she feels safe."

I stand from the stool. His shoulders sag slightly—the relief plain when he realises I'm not about to lay him out.

Again.

"Oh, and by the way," I add, turning back. "Having photos of someone else's girl? That's fucking creepy. So I took the liberty of deleting them. But don't worry—I replaced them with some lookalikes. Seems you've got a type. I'd be careful though, some of those girls look like jailbait. Be a shame if the police got wind of them."

His mouth drops open. The fear flashing across his face lights me up like the Fourth of fucking July.

"Enjoy prison, you sick son of a bitch," I say, my voice smooth, almost cheerful. "I hear they give special attention to guys who prey on women. Think of me every single time you feel as violated as you made her feel."

I wink at the fucker—because yeah, I'm a dick like that—then turn on my heel and walk out the door.

Back to my girl.

My reason.

Flawed

My salvation.

I shove the bar door open.

Don't look back. Let the stink of fear and stale beer rot behind me.

Cooler air slaps me in the face.

Cold. Sharp.

I don't feel it. I'm already somewhere else.

Already with her.

Boots hit gravel. Steady. Heavy. Each step pulls me closer.

Closer to what matters.

Closer to the only thing that fucking matters.

She is curled into the passenger seat like something breakable, my jacket drowning her small frame, the sleeves swallowed in her fists. Sunlight spills through the windshield, casting her in a glow and making her look too soft for a place like this. Her knees are tucked up tight, her chin rests just barely on denim, like she is trying to disappear, like the weight of the world finally got too heavy.

Her eyes find mine—wide, wary, beautiful. She looks like hope in a broken world, like something pure I have no business even breathing near. Jesus, an angel. She doesn't know. Doesn't know the blood I would spill, the lines I would cross, just to keep her safe.

I yank the door open and drop into the seat. No words. No questions. She doesn't need them—she already knows.

I reach for her—I can't help it. My hands, rough from everything I've done, go soft the second they touch her. I cup her face, thumb brushing her cheekbone, careful and steady. Like she's the only thing that makes sense anymore.

"You good, beautiful?" my voice is shot to hell, scraped raw by everything I'm trying not to say.

She nods, a tiny, brittle movement, and something inside me splits wide open at the seams. I shift the car into gear, one hand on the wheel, the other on her thigh, grounding me—anchoring me to the only thing that still matters.

She is my anchor. My reason for breathing.

◆ ◆ ◆

Flawed

I barely remember the drive.

All I know is one second I'm at the bar, the next I'm kicking the door to her—our—apartment shut behind us, scooping her into my arms like she's the only thing worth saving.

I don't say anything—not yet.

I just hold her.

She's exhausted, wrecked from the last few days, and it shows in every trembling breath.

Her face buried in my chest, her breath hitching against my skin, her fingers knotting into my shirt like she's afraid she will fall apart if I let go.

But I'm not going anywhere.

Not tonight.

Not ever.

I drop onto the couch with her still clinging to me, pull a blanket over us to make her feel more secure.

There's no questions asked. No explanations needed. I'm fairly certain she knows who I confronted in that bar but won't ask the question.

There's just the kind of silence that means everything when you've survived too much.

My arms tighten around her—holding together the pieces as I gently kiss the top of her head, a promise to keep her safe and a possessive branding.

"Mine," I breathe into her hair, so quiet she might not have heard me. "Always fucking mine."

When I'm confident she won't fall apart, I pick her up and carry her into the bathroom. I set her gently on the edge of the sink, careful like she's made of glass. Then I drop to my knees in front of her, my hands moving slowly as I untie her sneakers. It's such a small thing, barely takes a minute, but to me it feels like everything.

I kneel without thought, without hesitation, because that's what she does to me—brings me to my knees, makes me want to worship every inch of her.

It isn't weakness. It's instinct.

It's devotion.

I stand and turn the water to hot, the steam quickly filling the small room. I help her to her feet, steadying her when she sways. I've seen her in shock before, but this isn't that. This feels deeper. Like instead of shutting the world out, she's feeling every jagged edge of it—and

I'm fucking lost, scrambling to figure out how to be what she needs right now.

I strip her out of the rest of her clothes, slow and careful, guiding her into the stream of hot water. She barely reacts, just holds onto me like I'm the only solid thing left.

I peel off my own clothes without a second thought and step in after her.

Her arms snake around my neck, and she buries her face against my chest. I feel it, the way she draws strength from me, from the wreckage of everything I'm willing to be for her.

It damn near breaks me.

Gently, I peel her away from my body—hating the space between us—and start to wash her, slow and thorough, like I'm memorising every inch of her all over again. Like if I'm careful enough, I can scrub the weight of the world off her skin.

She's barely awake by the time I'm done, her body swaying on her feet. I wrap her up in a towel, tuck another around my waist, and guide her to the bed. She doesn't even make a sound, just folds into the mattress like she's been carrying too much weight.

I slide in next to her, not wanting to jar her. Still, I can't leave it alone.

I pull her across my chest, needing her closer, needing her breathing steady against me.

For the first time since leaving the pub, I let myself breathe too.

She's home.

She's safe.

She's mine.

CHAPTER 24

ALLY

I wake up feeling like I haven't slept at all.

The exhaustion runs bone-deep, not the kind a full night's rest can fix—the kind that comes from fighting battles you didn't even realise were still raging inside you.

Sunlight spills into the room, warm against the sheets. Jax is still wrapped around me, his hand heavy on my hip like even in sleep, he's scared I'll vanish.

I slip out of bed as quietly as I can, grabbing my phone from the nightstand.

I should be surprised to see a message waiting for me but the dozen missed calls raise alarm bells in my head.

Ty: Call me!

My heart stutters. I don't know if I'm ready for more news—good or bad—but I hit dial anyway, clutching the phone so tightly it might crack in my hand.

When he answers, his voice is tight yet happy? He doesn't sound right but he doesn't sound bad either

"How are you feeling?" he asks.

"I'm fine, what's up?" I whisper urgently, not wanting to wake Jax.

"Are you sitting down?"

"I'm not in the mood for games, spit it out."

"You need to sit down."

I plonk myself down on the end of the bed exasperated with his theatrics.

"Fine I'm sitting, what's up?" I whisper-shout.

"Why are we whispering?" he asks in a hushed tone.

"Because Jax is sleeping and if you don't spit it out,

next time I see you, I'll hand you your ass like I did when we were kids!"

He lets out a long exhale before speaking in a cautious tone. "Michael's been arrested."

The room spins violently and then stops too quickly making me dizzy. I lose feeling through my body and slip off the edge of the bed and land with a loud thump on the carpet.

"Ally?"

"I'm here. I heard you. I.."

I what? I don't know how to finish that sentence. "Stalking. Creating, possession and distribution of explicit material. Lots of it. He's done. Officially."

Goosebumps break out along my skin and I shiver.

"What… what explicit material?" I ask hesitantly.

I know he was stalking me but is the material of me? Fuck! What if it is.

"I don't know the full details, but… girls getting undressed and shit like that. Apparently, they are AI, but they're all young. So he's in a lot of trouble."

Jax grumbles something incoherent, catching my attention, before rolling over, smiling and then returning to lightly snore.

There's something about him that looks different.

I can't explain it but he looks content maybe? Validated?

The revelation hits me like a ton of bricks.

SON OF A BITCH!

Jax did this.

I don't know how but I know he is responsible.

"Ty I have to go," I rush out before ending the call before he has a chance to argue.

I take a moment to process what I'm feeling while staring at this beautiful—yet morally disturbed—man.

He smiles in his sleep again and I decide—I'm relieved.

Conflicted, yes. But, happy.

I pick myself up off the floor and climb over him, straddling his lap.

He stirs and slowly starts to stretch while opening his eyes, but he stops when he sees the expression on my face.

"What? He asks all cute and innocent—but can't hide the smirk that's breaking out across his gorgeous lips.

"Was it you?" I ask anyway, even though I already know the answer. I know exactly who made sure this happened, who fought my battles so I wouldn't have to.

He shrugs, all casual. "Might've been. Might not."

"You, are one scary motherfucker, Jackson Beckett!"

"I'll give you scary," he says, grinning. "But mothers aren't really my thing. Never understood the whole 'mummy issue' kink."

I throw myself down so my chest is against his, hiding my face in the crook of his neck.

"Thank you," I whisper against his skin.
For everything he's done.
For being the kind of man who would.

We stay like that for a long time, just breathing each other in. No words needed.

Eventually, I pull back enough to look at him, a smile tugging at the corners of my mouth.
"You know," I say, tipping my head up. "You might not like me so much now."

He raises an eyebrow, amused. "Oh yeah? Why's that?"

I grin, feeling lighter than I have in years.

"Because I'm about to get real boring. No drama. No stalkers. No broken pieces. Just… normal."

He lets out a low laugh, the sound rumbling through me like a promise.

"Beautiful," he says, cupping my face like I'm still something precious. "You could be boring as hell, and I'd still be gone for you."

Tears prick my eyes again, but this time, it's not sadness.

It's hope.

It's everything I thought I'd lost and somehow found again, standing right here in front of me.

"I feel like I could write a book with all the shit I've been through," I joke.

"You should. Or at least a bad joke. A Psychopath and trauma victim walk into a bar…" He pauses for dramatic effect and I break out in a fit of giggles, pressing my forehead to his chest

I smile and lean into him, breathing him in, letting the future wrap around us both.

For the first time, the future doesn't scare me. It feels like a gift.

Like home.

Because a psychopath and a trauma victim walked into a bar… and dared to stay.

Epilogue

JAX

"You need to relax," I bark, frustration spilling out of me.

"I'm trying!" she snaps back—but the tight ring of muscle just grips harder around the tip of my cock.

Took six goddamn months to talk her into letting me fuck her ass, and I'm blowing it before we've even really started. I'm too far gone, too lust-drunk on the idea of finally claiming the one hole that hasn't been filled with my come. I need to get a grip. Get control. Where the fuck is Sam when I need him?

I suck in a breath and reel it in.

Dropping my forehead to hers, I skim her cheekbone with my thumb and try again, softer this time. "Look at me."

She scrunches her nose, refusing to open her eyes.

I pull out completely and she collapses into the

mattress beneath me with a groan.

"Open your eyes, Beautiful."

"No," she fires back, like a tantrum-throwing toddler.

"Ally. Look at me."

Her eyes finally open and lock onto mine. I cup her face, my voice barely above a whisper. "There's my girl."

"Cut the crap, Jackson."

I huff. Without Sam, I've got nothing. She knows it.

"If I'm doing this," she says, glaring at me, "I'm doing it with *you*. Not him."

Fuck, this woman sees straight through every layer of bullshit I hide behind.

"We don't have to do it. You're the one who brought it up."

"I want to," she says, quieter now. Her cheeks flush pink.

"Then stop being so uptight and fucking relax."

"Fuck you! You'd be uptight too if I tried to do this to you."

And we're back to snapping.

"Why do you want this?" I ask, cocking a brow. "Is it

'cause you squirt when I use the plug?"

"I. DO. NOT." she says through gritted teeth—and I burst out laughing.

"Yeah, you do."

She doesn't answer, but her cheeks are flaming, and she won't meet my eyes.

"Use your words, Hannah."

I rarely use her real name, only when I'm teasing her but she doesn't mind it. The name Hannah no longer represents a prisoner of war. It's a badge she wears proudly now, a reminder of how far she's come.

"Because I want this with you," she mutters. "It feels more intimate than anything else we've done."

"It's hardly more intimate than when I caught you trying it on yourself with your BOB."

Her eyes narrow into slits. She's an angry kitten—more bark than bite—but I fucking love it.

"What's this really about?" I ask, softer. "Why the sudden interest?"

"I just want to feel close to you," she whispers like it's something to be ashamed of. And fuck, I melt.

I should've seen it coming. I've been watching her

for weeks, waiting for the cracks—I expected to find her curled in a ball in the shower violently rocking back and forward or clinging to me like a fucking koala. I did not think she would reach out through sex but it kind of makes sense.

My girl's a deviant.

With a new perspective, I shift my approach.

I cup her face and kiss the tip of her nose.

"You just need to relax," I say gently.

"You've done this before, right?"

"No," I lie.

"Really?" Her expression twists—half panic, half disbelief.

I sigh dramatically. "Of course I fucking have. But do you really want to talk about that right now?"

Her eyes narrow, then something fierce flickers in them. "Okay. I can do this."

I sit back, lube up again, and move over her, slow and steady.

I kiss her, sweet and unhurried, while I slide my fingers back in to stretch her.

"Just breathe, Beautiful. I won't hurt you."

She moans into my mouth.

I pull my fingers out and press the head of my cock against her tight, virgin hole.

"Deep breath."

Her chest rises against mine, and as it fills, I push in.

She shudders and clenches hard around me.

"Jesus fucking Christ. Don't do that," I grit through my teeth.

She clenches again and I nearly lose it.

I bite down on the need to come and refocus on her. Her eyes are squeezed shut, her mouth a perfect O.

"You okay?"

"Don't you dare move!" Her voice is high, breathy, on the edge.

I grab the clit sucker she loves and switch it on. The buzz makes her jolt.

I press it to her clit and she squeals, trembling. She's fucking close and I haven't even moved yet.

"You gonna come for me, Beautiful?" I whisper against her ear. "God, Ally. You take my cock so well."

"You gonna be my good girl and come with my cock in your tight virgin arse?"

She fucking detonates like never before—legs shaking, hips locking around me, mouth frozen in a silent scream.

I push in deeper, slow, just as she loosens her grip—and she comes again. Her body rides the wave, again and again, as I keep moving inside her, slow and steady.

Her pleasure's endless. And I'm not far behind.

The sight of her wrecked, the squeeze of her arse, the vibration of the clit toy—too much. My balls draw up, spine tingles, and I explode inside her.

She twitches beneath me, boneless.

"That was the most intense experience of my life," she mumbles.

"See?" I grin smugly. "Told you. Should've let me do it months ago."

She smacks my arm.

I kiss her tenderly, just in case getting her ass wrecked didn't give her the intimacy she's craving.

Then, true to form, she jumps up and bolts to the shower like her ass isn't still twitching—and I laugh at her flustered, adorable self-consciousness.

Flawed

◆ ◆ ◆

It's been six months.

Six months since everything imploded. Since lies turned to ash, since blood dried on knuckles and hearts were ripped out and handed back, still beating. Since we stopped pretending we weren't all kinds of fucked-up and started building something anyway.

And somehow, against every odd, it worked.

Ally's in the kitchen, standing at the counter in nothing but one of my old T-shirts and a pair of fluffy socks she insists aren't mine but definitely are. Her hair's up in one of those messy buns she swears isn't intentional, but I've seen her redo it three times when she thinks I'm not watching.

There's a half-eaten piece of toast on her plate, a coffee mug she forgot she made, and pages scattered everywhere—her manuscript, bleeding red ink and sticky notes. It's her second draft. Her story. Raw, brutal, honest. The kind of story that forces people to sit with their discomfort—and maybe walk away a little changed.

She's telling the world what they never saw. What they refused to see. The trauma. The survival. The quiet, invisible strength it takes just to keep breathing. And she's not hiding anymore.

She doesn't know I've read the whole thing. Twice. Every word branded into my memory. Some parts gutted me. Others made me want to drive to old addresses and finish what I've started. But I didn't. Because she asked me not to. And for her, I'm learning how to ask first.

Mostly.

"Stop hovering," she mutters without looking up, scribbling something on a margin like she's in a duel with her own sentences.

"I'm not hovering," I lie from a full two feet behind her, arms crossed, staring at the curve of her back through thin cotton.

She snorts. "You're breathing like you're about to commit a felony."

"Not about to. Just waiting for a reason."

She shakes her head, amused but not surprised. Nothing surprises her anymore. Not the darkness in me.

Not the possessiveness. Not the way I still wake up sometimes and reach for her like I'm afraid she disappeared.

And she's never once asked me to be softer.

She knows I don't do gentle unless it's with her. The rest of the world can rot—I'm done trying to be palatable. Ally's the only thing in this life that ever made me want to be anything better than what I was.

She turns around, finally meeting my eyes. There's something tired in her face—this kind of bone-deep weariness that's lingered since everything came crashing down. Some days, it still grips her by the throat. But she's stronger now. Not in that loud, warrior-shit way people like to romanticise. She's strong in the quiet, brutal way that looks like getting out of bed on days when it hurts to breathe. Like writing down the worst parts of her life so someone else might feel less alone in theirs.

"You okay?" I ask.

She nods, but the kind that means not really.

So I cross the room and pull her into me, no hesitation. Her head finds my chest like it always does, and I breathe her in—this perfect mix of vanilla, ink, and something I can only describe as her. My hands run over her back, grounding her, grounding me.

"I'm proud of you," I say quietly into her hair.

"You're biased," she mumbles into my shirt.

"Damn right I am."

She leans into the hold, lets herself sag a little. I don't think she even notices she does it anymore—like her body knows it's safe before her mind catches up.

She's exhausted. She's been reliving it all. The book. Therapy. Her past trying to claw its way into her present. All of it's taken a toll. And still—she's here. With me. Choosing this life we carved out of chaos.

"I still don't know how the hell this became our normal," she says after a beat, voice muffled.

"A psychopath and a trauma survivor walk into a bar…" I murmur against her temple.

"And stayed for the shit show," she finishes, dryly.

"Still the best punchline I've ever heard."

She snorts. "You're the worst."

I grin, brushing her hair back, tipping her chin up so she's forced to meet my eyes.

"And you're mine," I say, voice low and certain.

She rolls her eyes, but her smile gives her away.

"God, you're still such a possessive asshole."

"Yeah," I say, kissing her forehead, "but I'm your possessive asshole."

She sighs, dramatic as hell, and pulls away just far enough to reach for her manuscript. "Fine. But if this thing ever gets published and people ask what my inspiration was—"

"I expect full credit."

"You'll get a restraining order."

"Same thing."

She laughs, and it hits me in the chest like it always does—sharp, bright, and alive. That sound used to be rare. Now, I hear it every damn day. And I'll never stop being greedy for it.

So yeah. I still don't sleep much. Still have violent thoughts I don't say out loud. Still want to punch half the people she lets into her life. But she grounds me. And I protect her. And somehow, that's enough.

We're not perfect. Not even close.

But we're here.

And whatever comes next?

We'll face it together.

Because a psychopath and a trauma survivor walked into a bar… and somehow built a life from the wreckage.

Flawed

The End

Flawed

Also by Margaux Paris

Broken - Damaged Hearts 1

Flawed - Damaged Hearts 2

Wounded - A Damaged Hearts Story

Flawed

About The Author

Margaux Paris is a Sydney-based author of dark romance and emotionally charged contemporary fiction. A lifelong romance reader with a love for morally grey men, broken heroines, and stories that walk the tightrope between ruin and redemption, Margaux never imagined she'd one day be on the other side of the page. It wasn't until her husband gently nudged her to take a chance that she finally put pen to paper—and discovered that writing the book she could never quite find on the shelf was exactly where she was meant to be.

What started as a deeply personal passion project slowly evolved into the Damaged Hearts Duet, a raw, unflinching story about love, loss, obsession, and the complicated path toward healing. With Broken and Flawed, Margaux invites readers into a world of emotional chaos, layered characters, and love that doesn't always play fair—but always leaves a mark.

When she's not writing or sneaking in late-night reading sessions, Margaux is a proud mum to three wild

Flawed

and wonderful young boys who keep her on her toes (and her coffee intake dangerously high). Fueled by caffeine, V Energy Drink, and an ever-growing obsession with fictional men—Joey Lynch being the gold standard—she finds inspiration in the beautifully flawed characters that live in her head long before they make it to the page.

Margaux is currently working on Wounded, a spin-off in the Damaged Hearts universe that dives into the story of an emotionally repressed mechanic and the girl he never really let go.

Afterword

Thank you for making it to the end of Flawed.

This book was never meant to be neat. It was never meant to be soft. It was written for the ones who love too deeply, who break and rebuild, who know that sometimes love doesn't save you—it destroys you and still, somehow, it's worth it.

Jax and Ally's story has always been about more than romance. It's about control, surrender, trauma, survival, and what it means to find yourself in the wreckage of what someone else left behind.

If you saw yourself in these pages, if you felt something shift or ache or spark while reading—thank you. You were never alone in that.

To those who stayed with them through the fire: you are the reason stories like this are told.

Broken doesn't mean weak. And flawed doesn't mean unworthy.

-Margaux Paris

Flawed

Acknowledgments

Writing a book is a deeply personal process, but bringing one into the world takes a village—and I'm lucky to have had some of the best.

To my husband—thank you for enduring months of me talking about Jax as if he were real (because let's face it, he kind of is). For listening to my endless rants about morally grey men, complicated plot twists, and emotionally loaded scenes—thank you for always being in my corner, no matter how obsessed I got.

To my favourite book friend—you know who you are. Thank you for loving swoon-worthy fictional boyfriends as fiercely as I do and for being there through the chaos of the last few months. Your support, sarcasm, and late-night messages meant more than you know.

To my editor, CJ Editing—thank you for your patience and your urgency, in equal measure. For your hilarious feedback, for catching what I missed, and for treating this story with care and clarity. I'm so grateful.

To my incredible ARC readers—thank you for falling

Flawed

for Jax the way I did. Your early support, excitement, and kind words gave this book its heartbeat. Knowing he lived in your minds the way he lived in mine means everything.

And to you, dear reader—thank you for taking a chance on a story about love, trauma, obsession, and healing. I hope it stays with you long after the final page.

Flawed